To Donna,

Enjoy this Book!

Girl with Pencil, Drawing

Linda Maria Frank

Book Two in the Annie Tillery mystery series

iUniverse LLC
Bloomington

Girl with Pencil, Drawing

iUniverse books may be ordered through booksellers or by contacting:

iUniverse
1663 Liberty Drive
Bloomington, IN 47403
www.iuniverse.com
1-800-Authors (1-800-288-4677)

ISBN: 978-1-4917-1117-0 (sc)
ISBN: 978-1-4917-1119-4 (hc)
ISBN: 978-1-4917-1118-7 (e)

Library of Congress Control Number: 2013918820

Printed in the United States of America.

iUniverse rev. date: 11/1/2013

Contents

Francesca spied DicCristiani, When he turned to leave,
she said, "Please leave the building with me."

Chapter 1
The Saturday Art Class

The screech of iron wheels against iron rails trilled through my body, making my teeth ache. I tightened my knees against the large art portfolio as the New York City subway train lurched through a turn, slowing towards the Spring Street station. Not able to control my nervous energy, I left my seat and headed for the sliding doors. I balanced the precious portfolio between my knees and looked at my reflection in the door windows, checking for obvious defects in my appearance.

Boy, I thought, *You are nervous, girl. Let's see.*

I ticked off the usual list of suspects causing appearance problems, starting with the new haircut and highlights. I thought it made my face look thinner, and I liked it. *Check!* I used makeup this morning but hadn't hidden the sleepy eyes. *Who gets up this early on a Saturday? Well check, anyway.* My outfit, comprised of a black fitted jacket, black and white plaid scarf, and black earmuffs made my light hair and eyes pop. *Check!*

My mother's warning rang in my ears. "Annie, stand up straight! It makes all the difference in the impression you make." For once I didn't argue with that voice in my head. I squared my shoulders, lifted my chin, and grabbing the portfolio and backpack, braced for the jolting stop I was anticipating with excitement and dread. Doors opened silently amid the racket of the train station. As cold damp air crept into the car, the few early Saturday morning passenger traveling with me spilled out on the platform.

My legs had a life of their own, carrying me up the ancient grimy stairway to the street above. My first art lesson at the DiCristiani Galleries loomed ahead of me. All the confidence I had felt when I won first place in my high school's art contest evaporated like the steam swirling up from the manhole covers in the downtown streets of Soho. Here was my chance to prove the talents I hoped I had.

I was anxious to get started and most of all to meet my teacher. The gallery had sent a packet of information about their program of studies, the art studio, and my instructor, Francesca Gabrielli. Her credentials were impressive. The fact that she had been accepted in a program at the Metropolitan Museum here in New York was big.

They had sent me a brochure with photocopies of her work which I admired. I hoped to learn important techniques from her, and go beyond what I had learned in my high school studio art class.

This was going to be an exciting opportunity for me. I tightened my grip on my portfolio and remembering my "posture for success" pep talk, moved on down the street.

A fuchsia pennant hanging from a brownstone building furled and unfurled itself in the icy February wind. That brownstone with its steep flight of steps was my destination. Half a block away it posed as a haven from the cold. Even so, I wasn't sure that I wanted to make the short walk there. I'd have to open my portfolio and show my pieces in a place not likely to be so nurturing to a seventeen year old as my art teachers at Rhodes School.

I took the steps, two at a time, and pushed the heavy oak and leaded-glass door open. What a beautiful place! I admired the wood paneling, the black-and-white marble floor, the art pieces placed around the two-story entrance hall. There was no one around and I wondered where to go. No little signs with arrows posted around the room. The only logical place to go was to follow a hallway leading to the back of the house.

"No! I can't do that! It's . . ." The strong words stopped me like a wall. The female voice came from the only open door in the hallway.

"I'm not paying you to tell me . . ." shouted a deep male voice. I lost the rest of the sentence as his angry voice dropped.

The sign above the door said ART CLASS. I stopped, unsure what to do. My instincts prickled, sensing the electric tone of the conflict inside the room.

"You're hurting me!" shrilled the female voice.

With that I decided to barge in "Excuse me," I said smiling. "Oh, I'm sorry, I didn't mean to interrupt," I continued, staring at the man's hand still grasping the wrist of a young woman. She couldn't have been more than a few years older than I. In a rough gesture, he flung her arm away, tossing back a warning as he left. "I'll see you later." His emphasis was on the you.

"You must be here for the art class." Trying to hide her distress, she approached me with an outstretched hand. "I'm Francesca Gabrielli. And you are?"

"Anne Tillery." I grasped her cold trembling hand and I tried not to stare at the ugly red mark on her wrist. *What was this all about?* I thought, more than a little confused.

She withdrew her hand, struggling to gain control of herself.

"I'm your instructor today. Let's set you up and get started."

Francesca Gabrielli was a small person, probably not over five feet as compared to my five foot eight. She was pretty with large brown eyes and a mane of curly short dark hair. She really looked like an artist, white poet's shirt over black turtleneck and leggings. Curling down the back of her neck was one graceful curl bleached red and tied with a black ribbon. Large silver hoop earrings and black suede clogs completed the look. She was elfin in appearance. She could have been one of Santa's helpers, and this image just added to my confusion.

This was not at all what I had expected to happen on my first day. I felt anger at the man in the office. My curiosity went into full gear as I tried to make the impression of Francesca Gabrielli at my first meeting and her outstanding credentials fit with the ugly scene in the office.

Pushing these feelings aside and trying to concentrate on the task at hand, I followed Francesca. The studio was in the back of the house in a glass conservatory that must have been the by-gone owners' year-round indoor garden. That was the style when brownstones were built. The light was perfect. The glass classroom had an abundant supply of easels and small tables for paint and supplies.

"Pick your spot, Anne. You're early. I have to take care of something, but I'll be right back."

Francesca Gabrielli was shaken and pale as she left the room. My mind wandered as I set about arranging my materials. I wondered what danger, if any, my new instructor faced.

The model walked in taking his place on the stool in the middle of the conservatory. He was an old Asian man with long white hair and a deeply lined face. Automatically I began to plan my strategy for placing his image on my sketch pad. He presented a challenge.

The boy who had set up shop next to me quipped, "Hi. Fred's the name. Paint's the game."

I laughed and the Asian man offered some of his wisdom to Fred. "Yeah, and you should stick to paint, because your humor is from Oz, man." We all laughed at this unexpected comment.

"My name's Annie," I said, and along with the other students, began to concentrate on my work.

Another member of the class arrived, a tall girl who might have been Indian. She chose an easel on the other side of Fred. A fourth classmate joined us, introducing himself as Edward. Edward was an impressively tall African-American and set up next to me.

Francesca returned looking much better. She drew a deep breath, pulling her sleeve over her bruised wrist. "Since this is your first lesson here at DiCristiani's, I'd first like you to do your own thing. This way, I can judge where I need to help you." As she circulated from sketch pad to sketch pad she seemed to grow calmer. Our model sat very still, now giving forth purely oriental mystery. We coaxed his image out of our pads and pencils, while Francesca made comments, correcting technique, making suggestions about lighting and perspective. The time flew and I felt good, confidence building.

"You're doing real good there, Anne. You've got to have some talent to get a place here at Mr. D's."

Francesca's comment was music to my ears. I watched her as she browsed through my portfolio. She looked young, maybe nineteen or twenty, but was probably in her mid-twenties to have this job.

"Please call me Annie. I like that better." I ventured, "That's not a New York accent."

"No, I'm from Boston. I worked there for two years, so that I could come here. I'm working this job to pay for my own art lessons at the Metropolitan. There's more work here than in Boston. Lots of restoration work." She ran her fingers through her thick curly hair, pausing, seeming to weigh her words.

Turning back to me, eyes darkened by trouble, she asked, "Can you do me a favor when class is over, Annie?" Francesca was twisting an oily rag around her fingers, anxiety apparent in every fiber of her body.

What could I say? I thought.

"Sure, if I can," I replied, wondering if I would regret it, struggling again with the images of Francesca-the-instructor and Francesca-in-trouble.

"When class is over, I want to leave with you. I mean, you know, we can go out the front door together. I'll put my coat near your things, and we'll just go. Okay?" She waited for a response.

"Are you afraid of that guy who was trying to break your arm?" I asked, thinking it all too obvious.

"Yeah, that's Mr. D. We had a dispute about what's business and what isn't and I'm getting a little bored with his way of proving a point. The last time we didn't see eye to eye, the security guard showed up just in the nick of time. He saved me from what I suspect would have been unwanted facial reconstruction."

She rubbed her wrist absently and continued, "If I leave with you, he wouldn't dare to try anything. He looks into all the applications of the students who come here. You're a cop's kid, right?"

"My Aunt's on the New York City police force," I shot back. Her knowing about Aunt Jill unnerved me. Aunt Jill's work as a New York City detective has made her a careful and suspicious mother hen where I'm concerned. "Why don't you quit working here?"

"It's more complicated than that. Will you do it?" Again, that pleading look.

"Okay." I shrugged.

That's right, I thought, *He wouldn't dare try anything with me. I guess. What could happen to us in broad daylight?* When this "favor" was done, I would get Aunt J to see if she could find out more about Francesca Gabrielli, something more than the information on a brochure. I wanted to continue my lessons, but I also didn't want to feel that my instructor was in danger, especially if I couldn't help her. *Annie to the rescue,* I concluded, shaking my head.

The subject of our discussion stuck his head in the room at that moment, causing Francesca to take a pencil to my work, explaining, "This technique works best with the hair."

She never touched my sketch. Under her breath she murmured, "It's really good, Annie. When we have more time, I'll show you some neat tricks of the trade." She winked. We continued working on for about a half hour, putting finishing touches on our preliminary sketches.

The class ended, my heart soaring with her comment, and my knees shaking with the prospect of leaving this beautiful place in escape mode. We left the building fast, so fast that we were still slipping on coats as we fled down the steps. We headed for the subway station at a trot. As we passed a small alley, two men emerged and stepped out after us.

"Are they following us?" I inclined my head in their direction.

"You can count on it," Francesca replied stiffly.

"Look, I know the subways like the back of my hand, Francesca. If we can get on that platform, I can lose them." My art portfolio banged against my leg as we began to run. My cell phone was in my knapsack.

Oh, hell, I thought. *I couldn't get it out and run for the train at the same time. Why hadn't I put it in my pocket!*

"Let's go!" she said, face grim, pushing me forward.

The men followed. Taking out Metrocards to speed things along, we squeezed through the turnstile, racing for the stairs and the platform for the uptown train. The station began to rumble. "That's our train," I yelled.

We ran, catching sight of our two pursuers coming through the turnstile as we ducked down the steps. The car doors slid open just as we got to the platform. We pushed into the train. The doors didn't move for a heart-stopping minute as we watched feet, legs, torsos, and finally, the heads of those sinister forms appear on the stairway. We're trapped, I thought. The men were on the platform, heading for our car.

The doors closed! Francesca and I collapsed against each other, catching our breath. I managed to get the cell out of my knapsack, clicked it open and damn, no signal! What luck! This wasn't a station that had cell service. We got off at the next stop, changing trains as many times as possible. Finally, we emerged at 47th Street and headed for St Patrick's Cathedral. Once inside, we knelt together at one of the small side altars, feeling relatively safe. We had lost those guys.

"What kind of trouble are you in?" I demanded feeling entitled to an explanation. After the last half hour, I thought I deserved it.

"He wants me to do some copying for him. You know, works by famous artists."

"What's wrong with copies?" I asked, "As long as they're sold as copies."

"That's the trouble, Annie. I don't trust him. I think copy and forgery are the same for him. I think he's into some other illegal stuff as well. Why does a legitimate businessman need those thugs? They're mean dudes and he's trouble!" Francesca seemed vulnerable. She was away from home and in danger. I liked her, and I wanted to help her.

"Where do you live?" I asked.

"Above the gallery," she answered looking down at her hands.

"Uh, I don't think so, not any more!" I decided quickly. "Come home with me. I live with my aunt. She's cool." I felt good about this idea. "You can't go back there anyway." I added.

"I don't know. That gallery is my only connection with making it in the art world. It's my job. How will I live?" Francesca agonized.

"Good question. I've got to think about this."

We left the cathedral, heading uptown to my home. My mind was grinding away.

What if Francesca was not completely innocent of DiCristiani's illicit activities? Oh boy, this is complicated! Again my gut won out.

I wondered what I would tell Aunt Jill. I had a good relationship with my aunt but she was very cautious. I had to get it across to her how dangerous this looked without her deciding I shouldn't get involved. I couldn't let Francesca go back to that gallery. My instincts told me she was worth the trouble. Maybe it would be Annie and Aunt J to the rescue.

Snow had begun to dust down from the gray February sky. With a heavy heart, I wondered what would happen to my Saturday art classes.

Chapter 2
ANNIE'S HOUSE GUEST

WE TRUDGED ALONG THE BUSY street, blinking away the tears born of the frigid wind. My mind ground away in maximum overdrive sifting through various arguments I would use to convince my aunt that this new-found friend at my side should come to stay with us. At least until she escaped from the trouble she was in. After all, this person was my art instructor and a superior one, at that. If I were to develop my talent, I needed to protect her. I needed to work all this out right now and then I'd call my aunt. I was always good at giving myself pep talks. Would Aunt J agree?

"Look, Annie, I'm going to try to get a room somewhere. I don't feel right just barging in on you and your aunt like this." Francesca broke the silence of our three block walk from St Pat's. Hands jammed into her parka, head bent to the wind, she stopped suddenly.

"I've got to go back for my stuff. I don't even have the phone number of a friend to call."

Derailed from my train of thought, I was shocked by her change of heart.

"How can you even think of going back there?" I gasped.

I didn't know whether I felt more hurt that she didn't think I was a friend she could call, or just stunned that she could go back there to face a man who obviously had an attitude of big dimensions where she was concerned. I felt my face go red as she backed away from me, determination jutting from her small jaw.

"Annie, if I'm going to move out of DiCristiani's, I've got to get my belongings. I just can't leave everything there."

Logic kicked in. *What could I do? I couldn't hold her prisoner. I'd forgotten my Junior Crime Solvers' handcuffs.*

"Okay, Francesca." I felt my shoulders droop with the realization that she was a stranger and that this is a free country. A little person inside me whistled a sigh of relief. Aunt J might have been a hard sell on this one and now I wouldn't have to tangle with her.

Francesca wheeled on the toes of her sturdy work boots and began to dodge through the crowd on 47th Street. I watched her go, anxiety finally overcoming relief.

"Wait, Francesca!" I yelled, running after her. I tripped over the legs of a dozing homeless man who was sitting in a doorway. His container of coins and bills scattered all over. "Oops, sorry," I shouted over my shoulder.

The guy woke up, saw what happened and started after me. I wanted to help him pick up the coins, but I had to get to Francesca. *At least I hadn't stepped on his lunch.* I ran after her, trying to put some distance between me and the homeless man who was shouting all kinds of nasty things at me.

After I had gone a few yards I felt something hit my back. On God, I muttered, "What was that? I turned half expecting to see the homeless guy with another object, ready to throw at me. Instead I saw the remains of his cup of cold chili that had broken and erupted down the back of my jacket. I suppose I should have been grateful. It's only chili.

Up ahead, Francesca was stuck at a crosswalk, traffic badly snarled. A traffic cop in the middle of it held up her hand and whistled for the traffic coming from Francesca's direction to stop. She was forced to wait, allowing me time to catch up to her. As I grabbed her arm from behind, she attempted to give me a karate kick, stopping in mid-air when she recognized me.

"It's no use, Annie. I've got to take care of some stuff. I'll call you." She shrugged away from me.

"You don't have my number," I reminded her.

"I'll get it from the art gallery files," she countered.

"Are you going to ask DiCristiani to look it up for you before or after he beats you up?" I asked sarcastically.

"I'm not stupid, Annie," she shot back, losing a little of her spunk in light of what DiCristiani could do to her.

"Let me give you my number now," I said, seizing the opportunity to stall for time to think. As I wrote down my home number, J's work number, and my address, inspiration finally caught fire.

"Do what you have to do. But, if you don't call me by four today, I'm calling in some heavy duty reinforcements. I'll ask my aunt to put a trace on you. It won't be official, because it takes forty-eight hours to file a missing persons report. But, she'll pull strings." I crossed my fingers behind my back.

Francesca's shoulders sagged. "I can't afford to have cops in on this. DiCristiani can get me into deep trouble." She looked off into the distance, chewing her lip, her steamy breath wisping away in the breeze. When she looked back, she seemed to have made up her mind about something. The soft Madonna-like face was set, hard and dark, like the frozen slush piles on the side-walk.

"I'm going to take care of business," she said quietly, "and then, I'll call."

"I want your phone number too, just in case." I pushed.

"No! You'll have to trust me. I can't get anyone else involved in this. Look, I'm sorry I asked you to help. You did, and now it's over for you. I'll take care of the rest."

Giving up, I took off for home, weaving and dodging through the crowds in the street, feeling snow drift down the neck of my jacket.

Chapter 3
Taking The Bull By The Horns

I STAMPED MY FEET AT the intersection of 7th Ave. and 60th St. The light changed and I trotted across the street, moving quickly to keep warm. The snow was steady now, sifting down in rippling curtains from a sky that was too dim for mid-afternoon. I tucked my free hand into my armpit and trudged on, head bent to the wind.

In the last three blocks, I had convinced myself that Aunt J was going to help Francesca. She wouldn't let somebody like DiCristiani get away with beating up on someone like her. I was going to have to soften her up first though by laying it on pretty thick. I ran though my mind just what had happened today. I realized that I wasn't going to have to pad this story at all. Aunt J was going to go nuts when she heard this. She might even insist that I quit the art class. *What a dismal thought!* Maybe I needed to downplay what happened. Losing the art class was not at all what I wanted.

A breeze bearing the irresistible aroma of roasting chestnuts tossed a spate of snow flakes into my eyes. It was getting colder, and I was starving with another long ten city blocks to go. I stopped at a little umbrella stand and bought a bag of chestnuts and a cup of hot chocolate.

Crouching in a store entrance, I wolfed down my snack thinking, thinking, thinking. My hunger eased, and as my mind cleared I knew that only the truth would work in this situation. I didn't need to make it worse. It was already pretty bad and I had better not hide the truth. Someone could get hurt, namely Francesca. Or me!

Ten blocks later, Mickey, our apartment house doorman, let me into the luscious warmth of the lobby. In a minute the elevator stopped at our floor and I flung myself through the door into our homey rent-controlled three-bedroom apartment. The cold finally won out and I ran for the bathroom.

Aunt J wasn't home. There were no messages on the answering machine, no notes. Good. That meant she'd be home by five.

The intercom buzzed. It was Mickey. He forgot to give me the mail. I told him to send it up on the elevator. When I went to retrieve the mail I saw a package for me on top of the pile of mail on the elevator floor. The return address said, DiCristiani Galleries. I looked around warily as I went back inside our door. I felt very jumpy. *She better call at four,* I thought, as I realized that the package had to have been mailed, at the very latest, yesterday. I wasn't "in trouble" yesterday. I tore it open.

Two large books on art techniques made up the bulk of the contents. There was a thick sheaf of papers as well, which at first glance, appeared to be lessons and homework assignments. There was a letter too.

Dear Ms. Tillery,

Welcome to DiCristiani Galleries. To make your art lessons and experience with the Art School more meaningful, we have included lessons, exercises and texts. You will find them a valuable adjunct to your actual classroom experiences. Your instructor will be Ms. Francesca Gabrielli, a talented apprentice with our gallery. Your class will be in the conservatory at the rear of the gallery. If you have any questions please call us, and good luck.

Our Staff

This should have arrived before today, I surmised. I flipped to the first assignment, wondering if I'd failed to prepare for the class I had just completed; maybe a refresher course in crisis intervention, evasion tactics or urban guerilla tactics. No, there was no prep, just homework. I turned to the books, and browsing through them, I became absorbed in a chapter on portrait painting, checking to see if my sketch of the Asian man was on the right track.

Before I looked up again, I heard the key in the door and Aunt J came through the door laden with a delicious smelling parcel. I recognized the mix of garlic and spices as Chinese food.

"Hi Annie! Like the snow?" inquired Aunt J taking off her coat.

My Aunt J was a petite woman. In her early forties, she projected an air of quiet confidence. Her face was handsome, not pretty, with large intelligent blue eyes. She would stand out in a crowd as someone you wanted on your side. She always made me feel secure in a world where things could change in a second.

"Yes! It's great," I replied, feeling somewhat distracted.

Aunt J came close to me, putting her hands on my shoulders which meant she had to reach up. I looked into those clear blue eyes marveling at the tricks of DNA. Both my dad, who was J's brother, and my mom had those clear blue eyes. Mine were gray-green. Mom had once told me, before she started to drink so much, that my grandmother, whom I never knew, had eyes that same color. I wasn't as fair as my aunt. My hair was more honey than blonde. My dad called us Mutt and Jeff because she was short and I was tall. We did have that same "I'm smarter than I look" expression though. I guess we were smarter than we looked. Did that mean we had brains and beauty? I never could figure that one out. Did it really matter?

I looked at the clock. It was five. Francesca hadn't called. I'd lost track of time and Aunt J was now staring at me as I gaped at the clock.

"What's up, Annie?" She followed my gaze to the clock. "The big hand is on the twelve, and the lit . . ."

"I had an interesting day today," I interrupted and dove in with my sweetest most endearing smile. "My art class turned out to be quite a little adventure and I need a big favor, Auntie."

She looked at me with that unwavering gaze that must have made her "clients" in the crime world very uncomfortable. "Are you hungry? Can we talk over dinner?"

"Yeah, I'm starved," I replied tearing into the package as she pulled dishes from the cupboard.

After we popped morsels of General Tso's chicken into our mouths, I started at the beginning and plowed through my story. When I got to the subway escape, Aunt J put down her chopsticks and walked to the window.

"I should have checked out the gallery owners," she muttered staring down at the street sights below, hands jammed in her pockets and shoulders hunched. "I figured any place Rhodes recommended would be okay. I try not to be a paranoid cop." Aunt J was obviously upset.

She turned to me looking very troubled. "Her credentials seemed okay. What do we really know about her?"

"She's from Boston. She's working at the gallery to pay for her art classes at the Metropolitan Museum. She's gotten herself mixed up with the wrong man. I like her. You will too." The words tumbled out, the last phrase a plea. "She should've called by now to tell me how she made out with DiCristiani. I'm worried, J."

"Why did she go back, Annie? That's what bothers me about her. If he's so intimidating, why is she so unwilling to just walk out, or file a complaint with the police? There are other jobs out there."

Aunt J had hit the nail on the head. The same thoughts were bothering me about Francesca. I didn't know how to answer her questions.

"I told you," I said quietly, feeling my heart sink with her analysis, "He pays her well for the copies she makes of master works." I looked at the floor realizing how shaky, and yes, shady, this whole explanation sounded.

Aunt J shook her head, getting that analytical look on her face. She continued, "But now she thinks that he may be selling them as authentic pieces? I don't get it, people who pay a lot of money for art, usually know about the subject. I would think that they would expect some proof of authenticity. I know I would."

Tapping her temple she paused for a second. "Provenance! That's what it's called," she cried out suddenly.

"What? What are you talking about?" I was very edgy now. The strange word and her triumphant yell had startled me.

"Art pieces of great worth are usually sold with a paper verifying their authenticity, called a provenance, pronounced in the French way," stated Aunt J.

"Maybe someone else is forging proven . . . , what's that word, for DiCristiani as well," I offered.

"There are so many questions here, Annie."

"Well, if we could get Francesca here, you could ask her," I suggested grasping at straws.

"You're right," Aunt J stated flatly. "And that's what we're going to do, question her. She's obviously in a dangerous situation, young and in trouble. Plus I don't want you going back there . . . ,"

"But J!" I protested.

"Until I clear this up." She shushed me. "They know that you helped her. Where do you think that leaves you, Miss Anne Tillery? How old did you say she is?"

I thought about it, remembering Francesca's face, the beautiful clear skin. Aunt J had once explained how lines and wrinkles give away age. Despite the flawless skin, Francesca had to be in her twenties to have accomplished as much schooling and work experience as stated in her credentials.

"Six or seven years older than me." I answered.

Aunt J looked at her watch. "Seven o'clock," she mused. "Lt. Red is on tonight. I'll call and have him start running some checks on these people." She headed for the phone, but before she could pick it up from its cradle, it rang.

"J here." I often wondered why she didn't answer the phone, Detective Tillery here, instead of just "J here." I asked her once and her reply was, "Those who need to get in touch with Detective Tillery know that I'm J. Those that don't, don't need to know my profession," explained my ever-careful aunt.

"It's for you." She handed the phone to me, mouthing Francesca's name. I grabbed it. "Francesca! Where are you?" I demanded.

"I'm in police custody, Annie. Was that your aunt I was talking to? Maybe she can help me," pleaded Francesca.

"What happened?" I gasped. "Why are you in police custody?"

"DiCristiani was murdered this afternoon," she stated, a tiny quiver creeping into her voice. "I'm being held for questioning," She sobbed.

Chapter 4
Prime Suspect

"HANG ON, FRANCESCA." I PUT my hand over the mouthpiece. "DiCristiani's been murdered. She's at headquarters, J. They're questioning her about it. Can we help her?"

Aunt J recovered in a second. "Tell her we'll be right there. Tell her not to . . . Forget it! I'm not her lawyer."

"We'll be right there," I told Francesca, hanging up the phone. I tried to shake off the shock.

"Full Arctic gear Annie. It's a blizzard out there."

I love snow, but I couldn't get excited. Did Francesca have anything to do with this murder? Her last words to me that afternoon were ringing in my ears. She had said she needed to "take care of business." Well, murder was one way.

No, no, it couldn't be. I shook that thought right out of my head.

"Let's hurry, J. She must be so scared. She couldn't have done it." Our eyes locked for a second. I could see that Aunt J wasn't so sure.

The Toyota's front-wheel drive grabbed in the deepening snow at the curb as we emerged from the underground garage. The trip downtown was quicker than usual, made possible by the lack of auto traffic the snow had kept off the street. The city was transformed. Broadway was truly the Great White Way. Trees ordinarily not visible against the gray buildings stood out with branches festooned in swaths of white snow. Headlights and street lamps became tunnels of dancing flakes. Pedestrians were anonymous in layers of their warmest clothes looking like polar bears and Eskimos.

We arrived at police headquarters, parking right in front. J stuck her Police Benevolent Association shield on the dash and we hurried inside. A brief conversation with the desk sergeant allowed us to be escorted down a corridor to an interrogation room. As we entered the maze of offices, I spotted the top of Francesca's head. Signaling to Aunt J, we made our way in that direction.

She sat there clutching a cup of steaming liquid, looking small and cold. She had somehow lost her boots, and had an oversized pair of white sweat-socks on her tiny feet

"Francesca, we're here."

She looked up at me, then at Aunt J.

"I didn't do it." She stated earnestly, trying to get her quivering lip under control.

A police officer made his way over, his jacket off, service revolver in full view. A sight I'd seen so often, once familiar, now seemed menacing. Aunt J had a few words with him, out of ear-shot, once gesturing to Francesca's feet. He left, leaving the two of us alone with Francesca.

"Francesca, I'm Jill Tillery, Annie's aunt. I'm a police officer and you may be in a lot of trouble. If I can help you I will, but you must tell me everything you know."

Stop beating around the bush, J, I thought sarcastically.

Her frankness cut right through to Francesca. "Yeah, I know," she managed, looking down at her feet.

"Annie told me about your day today and I have lots of questions. But first, let's hear why you're here. Why do the police suspect you? I want to hear your story from beginning to end."

It was the professional Jill Tillery now. She took out her note pad and looked at Francesca, waiting.

Francesca looked back, fear written all over her pretty face. She pushed a lock of hair off her face with a shaking hand and clearing her throat, began to tell her tale.

"After I left Annie, I went to DiCristiani's apartment. He's on the Hudson River, nice place, with a view of the river. He's got bucks."

"I don't understand." Aunt J stopped her. "Annie said that it looked like he was about to slap you around this morning. Weren't you afraid?"

"I was making copies of masterpieces for him. When I started, he had me convinced that it was strictly legit. He really kissed up to me at first. He told me how good my work was." Tears leaked from the corners of her eyes. She squeezed them shut.

"How did you first meet?" Aunt J persisted.

"There was an ad on the students' bulletin board at the Met where I take art classes. The ad was for the instructor's job at the gallery. The salary was more than I was making as a guard at the Met. I answered the ad." Francesca squirmed in her chair, an involuntary shudder making her jerk.

"Did DiCristiani interview you?" She was making notes on her pad.

"Yeah, he took me out to lunch, was very charming. It made me really nervous. I figured he wanted to add a romantic twist to the job. He told me that the job might entail other 'little services' besides the lessons. I asked him, what kind of little services."

"What a sleaze," I muttered. The story became even more dramatic when told in Francesca's own words.

"It's important that you tell all of it, Francesca," urged Aunt J softly.

"He said he wanted me to do restoration work, maybe some copies. He showed me a masterpiece in an art text book, famous because the original is missing, supposedly stolen back in the 1800's. I was familiar with the story."

"He was impressed with what I knew, and told me to make what I would consider, as authentic a copy as I could."

"I was so relieved I had avoided his creepy hits on me, I said, sure. Besides, I pride myself on being able to copy almost anything."

Aunt J made a face. "Oh course, he loved your work, and you've been copying for him ever since," she concluded sarcastically.

"That's how I got here," Francesca agreed, explaining that he had paid her two thousand for each copy. I could knock one out every three months, including the aging process used to make it look like an antique.

"He told me he was selling the copies to people who had offices they used to impress their clients. Doctors and lawyers, stock brokers. Sounded good to me. But his choice of works always seemed odd to me."

"Odd, how?" interrupted Aunt J.

"The works that I was copying were all obscure, hard to find in texts."

"How did he pay you?"

"Cash. I'd go to his apartment. The outer door would be open. I'd go into the foyer. The money was in an envelope placed in a basket on a small table. It was spooky. I never saw anyone there."

"I'm sure there was some kind of surveillance. Nobody leaves that kind of money in a foyer with the door unlocked in New York."

"At first I didn't care what he did with the paintings. I needed the money. It was very easy for me," Francesca continued.

"And you changed your mind?" asked Aunt J.

Francesca didn't respond.

"Why did he become so nasty to you?" I asked. "You said he was charming at first. What happened?"

"I asked him if I could see one of my paintings hanging in someone's office. He said it was out of the question. I didn't leave it at that. I tried to find out who his customers were by going through his desk at the gallery. He caught me. He threw me against the wall, and I swear he would have killed me if the security guard hadn't walked in. That was last week.

I managed to avoid him until this morning, when you walked in on us."

"What did he want?" I asked. "At the gallery, when I interrupted your fight with Di Cristiani, you said, 'I can't do that.' What did he want you to do?"

Aunt J cleared her throat, nudging me.

"Oh, sorry. I didn't mean to interrupt," I said, turning red.

I backed off, but Francesca's account of DiCristiani's behavior was so awful, I was impatient to find out what happened next.

"He said he needed two paintings by the end of the month. I told him that I couldn't do it. He threatened he would call the police and say that I stole money from the gallery."

"Didn't you think it strange that he was so anxious for you to do those copies?" Aunt J said, frowning.

"Yes, I did. That's when I began to become suspicious about the copies. I thought maybe he'd sold them as the real thing. If he paid me two thousand dollars, he must have been getting a lot for them."

"Why didn't you go to the police?" I asked.

"I needed the job. I needed the money. I told you, I'm on my own here. My family can't send me to schools to get the kind of art education I want."

"That leaves the big question of why you went to see him today." Aunt J said quietly.

"I wanted to stop making the copies. But I didn't want to lose the job. I was going to promise my silence for my job. I would have tried to convince him that it is not in my best interests to rat on him because that would have implicated me. He also owed me money."

"What happened when you got there?" Aunt J prodded.

If I sat more on the edge of my seat, I'd be on the floor. Aunt J and I waited as Francesca cleared her throat to continue.

"The outside door was open as usual. I went in, intending to knock on the inside door. No need. It was ajar. There was no sound when I first came in. I stood for a second wondering what to do. Then I heard a door close somewhere inside, so I decided to go in. I called out his name, but as soon as I stepped inside, I saw him lying across his desk, blood dripping from a puddle around his head onto the carpet."

She shuddered, fingers white as they gripped the coffee mug. She sucked in a deep breath. The blood drained from her face, and she put her head on her lap to keep from fainting. Waiting a few seconds Aunt J asked, "What did you do then?"

"I'm not sure. I must have gone over to him, maybe not to him, but to get to the phone. That must be where all the blood on my boots came from. They took my boots," she said looking at J. "Will I get them back?"

"I don't think so," responded Aunt J. "Not until they clear you. They're part of the crime scene now."

Francesca took in the news, and continued even more gravely. "I must have walked through the puddle. I picked up the phone, but it was dead. Before I knew it, the maintenance man came in, looked around, and ran out. I guess he called 911 from somewhere else. He said that I was screaming like a banshee. I don't remember that either. All I know is I'll never forget his face, his head." Francesca's shoulders heaved as she finally gave into her sobs.

"What's going to happen now, J?" I asked, trying to console Francesca with a hug.

I tried to imagine being in her place. I was afraid for her.

"I have to talk to the investigating officer or someone from the crime scene unit, to see if her story jibes with what they have. If they don't have anything solid, they'll have to release her. She hasn't been arrested, just brought in for questioning."

Aunt J turned to Francesca. "Last question. Does anyone else know about the bad blood between you and DiCristiani?"

"I don't know," Francesca responded openly.

With that Aunt J left to get her answers. Francesca looked into my eyes, pleading. "I didn't do it, Annie," she repeated. "Someone has to believe me. I don't have anyone else."

"I believe you," I replied, crossing my fingers behind my back, hoping I was right. Remembering the many conversations I had heard over the years, I asked, "Did you touch anything besides the phone?"

"I don't think so, but I'm not sure."

"Did you see a gun?"

"Yes. The gun was in his hand."

"Did he commit suicide?" I was confused.

"They said it was murder. Maybe the murderer put the gun in his hand."

Aunt J had returned. "No prints on the gun, not even his. The gun was placed in his hand after death," she offered.

"That's how they know it wasn't suicide," I told Francesca.

"They've taken Francesca's boots and her fingerprints. She's free to go with us, under my recognizance, until the lab reports come back. Annie, ask the woman police officer if Francesca can borrow a pair of shoes. Tell her I'll bring them back."

As I left to get the shoes, my head was reeling from Francesca's gripping account of trying to side-step DiCristiani's advances to make good money, only to find out that she was involved in something so criminal and dangerous.

Aunt J was in command now. I heard her as I came back into the room with a pair of sneakers.

"Francesca, listen to me. You're going home with us. You're not under any kind of arrest, but it's best that I always know your whereabouts. Do you understand? If you violate that trust, you're on your own."

Francesca shook her head adamantly. "Thanks. I can't thank you enough. Thanks," she murmured, still shaking all over.

Chapter 5
Shady Characters

I opened my eyes and quickly shut them again. Brilliant sunshine filled my room with painfully dazzling light. I tried again. This time I could keep my eyes open, and I surveyed the space between our building and the one next to it. Through the window above my bed the small patch of sky was blue, but some sparkly crystalline stuff floated on an updraft toward the roofs. I remembered the snow! Jumping out of bed I ran into the living room to see how much snow had fallen during the night.

I crossed to the picture window, nearly stepping on Francesca. I'd forgotten that she was bedded down in the dinette on my air mattress.

"Morning, Annie." Aunt J was already in the kitchen fussing with the coffee maker. A faint sizzling from the range grew louder, the oven ticking as it expanded through the preheating cycle. All of this pointed to a big Sunday breakfast.

"Mornin, J." I opened the front door, and bent to pick up our *New York Times*, trying to keep the many pieces of it from falling all over the place.

"Turn to the City Section, Annie. See if our story made the paper."

I found the story, featured on the page usually devoted to city crime. *Manhattan Business-Man Found Slain in Chelsea.*

"Read it," urged my aunt.

"*John DiCristiani, a wealthy business man, whose financial interests reached as far as Hong Kong and Istanbul, was found shot to death in his posh apartment overlooking the Hudson River.*"

"*Mr. DiCristiani's body was found by an employee from his Soho gallery. The police questioned the employee, Ms. Francesca Gabrielli, at headquarters, but subsequently released her. Police would only confide that the murder weapon was found at the scene and that all other leads were being investigated. Mr. DiCristiani is survived by a son, Mark, twenty-five, a law student at New York University.*"

There was a news file photo of DiCristiani at some social function. Next to his picture was another of a young man, snow swirling around his head. The caption read*: Mark DiCristiani, son of the deceased, leaves the Medical Examiner's office.* I stared at the picture. He had the look of a male model. His eyes penetrated as they stared from the page. I wondered if he fit into this mystery.

"I see I made the paper," observed Francesca. Aunt J had tuned on the local TV news station. After the usual post-mortem, recapping last night's snow storm, the newscaster launched into an account of the DiCristiani murder. He led into a taped interview with the detective in charge of the case, Frank McDonnell. The screen switched to the interview.

"In your opinion, is the murder a drug-related robbery gone bad, Detective?"

"No sir, there was no evidence whatsoever of break-in or robbery. Nothing was disturbed. A considerable amount of money was found in the apartment as well. We are looking for other motives."

"What about the employee you questioned last night, Detective?"

"She's been released."

"Has she been cleared, then?"

"No one's been cleared yet, sir. This interview is over."

"We hear Mr. DiCristiani has a son . . ." the reporter insisted competing with the chatter of other reporters.

"Well, nothing new there," commented Aunt J, cracking eggs into a frying pan.

"After we eat, let's go for a walk in Central Park," I suggested. "We all need to clear our heads and work off all these calories."

J cleared her throat, an emphatic indication to me she was about to lay down the law. She didn't let me down. In her usual logical manner, she proceeded, "We need to define what 'under my recognizance' means, ladies. You may go about the business of your job or profession, but you must be accessible to me by cell phone. At other times you must be accompanied by me or someone I have assigned to you. In this case, it is Annie. God help you if you mess this up, because then, it's the electronic bracelet, or, as the case unfolds, something worse."

"Otherwise it's a good idea for the two of you, but I have some work that I have to clear up downtown. You two should see what you can brainstorm about the DiCristiani crime scene and fill me in when I get back. I still have a lot of questions." J delivered her ominous message as she passed around the steaming plates of food. I passed out glasses of orange juice and we ate our breakfast in silence, thinking about what she had just said.

The weather turned partly cloudy again with occasional flurries. The temperature hovered at around thirty, but there was little wind. We set off cross-town and soon the park opened up between the buildings. We crossed Central Park West and we started across the street to enter Central Park, but Francesca yanked me back toward the curb. As I looked up to see why, a cyclist who nearly hit me, sprayed a rain of slush all over the two of us. The cyclist kept going, crashing through another slushy puddle at the next corner.

"Those guys are a menace to anyone on foot," Francesca muttered, brushing herself off.

We entered the park, the landscape transformed into a wonderland for walkers, sledders, cross-country skiers, and skaters. Moving fast to keep warm, we headed towards the skating rink. Whatever had melted in the morning sun was freezing up again, glistening in the sporadic bursts of sunshine.

"Francesca?" The word streamed out of my mouth in a wisp of condensation that hung above her head momentarily like the balloons in comic strip conversations. Francesca looked up.

"Tell me everything you know about DiCristiani. Start with the gallery. I can't picture a guy who acts like a creep, and is involved in art fraud, being the sponsor of an art school."

"That's easy," Francesca stated, her face setting into a hard mask that matched the icy landscape. Her voice cracked as she began. "DiCristiani doesn't own the gallery. He manages it, uh, managed it. The gallery is owned by a German woman by the name of Helriegel. She is an old woman who has many contacts in Europe. She gets most of the art pieces for the gallery."

"How come she has somebody like DiCristiani run the gallery? Is she a shady type too?"

"No. She is quite the lady. And she has a grandson who is some hot looking dude," replied Francesca, lightening up with this last disclosure. "These people are very different from DiCristiani and his son. They have class, real upstanding types. That's certainly more than we can say for the deceased and his handsome son," she added with a wry twist of her mouth.

"Do you see them at the gallery often?"

"No, every once in a while. I've talked to Paolo. He's the grandson. They sponsor the art classes, not DiCristiani. The truth be known, I run those classes single-handedly. Paolo looks in on the operation for his grandmother."

"Paolo, that's not German," I said.

"You're right. Paolo is an Italian name, like mine. I don't know how it figures. People do cross the borders in Europe, you know."

I tried to organize this cast of characters in my head, and picture them as Francesca described them. She had a talent for painting a verbal portrait. There was DiCristiani, the shady deceased manager of the art gallery, followed by Frau

Helriegel, the absentee owner of that gallery, who was, as far as we knew, a fine up-standing citizen. The latest addition was Paolo, young, handsome and rich.

"How old is he?"

"Oh, I'd say twenty-three or four. He's a medical student."

"That answers my next question. I wondered why Paolo didn't manage the gallery. He's a little busy with school, I'd say. Why doesn't his grandmother, what's her name, run the gallery herself?"

"I think she's too old. She only comes in when there's a delivery of a new piece from Europe. She likes to see it on display, and tell DiCristiani what price it should command. She even has a bookkeeper work with him on the money end of the business."

"The paper said DiCristiani is a wealthy business man. What does he do?" I asked. The whole thing was getting too complicated for me.

Francesca looked sheepish. "I never trusted him, so I poked around at his desk every chance I got. He seemed to be an importer. That's probably how he got into the art field. I have a feeling that I didn't see much of the paperwork dealing with his other business ventures. Most of the correspondence I saw had to do with the gallery. I did see a couple of invoices for teak furniture from Hong Kong, and rugs from Istanbul, though. There were lots of phone numbers, some names and lists of numbers and letters that seemed to be serial numbers or something, nothing that told me a heck of a lot about him."

"Do you remember any of the names?" I pressed. "That could be important. Aunt J might be able to pass them on to the detectives handling the case."

"I'd have to think. They were mostly Italian and German. I do remember that."

"Why didn't you go to college in Boston, and live with your family? You could have saved money that way," I asked suddenly, realizing that Francesca was very young to be doing what she was doing. I tried to imagine myself, on my own, earning my own way a few years from now.

"I told you. Money," she stated frankly, lifting her chin slightly. "Plus the opportunities are here in New York, much more than in Boston."

Instantly embarrassed, I tried to soften the impact of my question. "Don't get me wrong. I admire you for going after what you want, and having the confidence to be on your own." After a short uncomfortable pause, I added, "I'm sorry."

"No! It's okay. There were ten kids in my family. My father was a Boston transit motor-man. He moonlighted as a security guard. Only three of us wanted college. But by the time my turn came, he was out of work on disability from a car accident. The others are in no position to help me financially. So here I am. If I stayed home and worked, I'd end up giving all my money to my mother. This way they don't have to support me, and I use my salary for school.

This job pays for lessons at the Met. It even saves me the cost of getting a laptop. I use their computers. The Met will get me contacts to do restoration work or legitimate copies. Those jobs will pay my tuition at night school. I'll make it." She smiled jauntily. "That's if I beat the murder rap," she snorted with more bravado than I imagined she felt. I liked Francesca. She couldn't have murdered that creep, DiCristiani. We had to help her.

Impetuously, I hugged her. "We'll find out who killed DiCristiani, Francesca. You have to tell Aunt J everything you've told me. She has a way of sorting out the facts." As we resumed walking, I noticed a man who had been leaning on a tree. He pushed off the trunk and took off behind us. For a moment, it made me nervous. But what could happen to us in this crowded park?

"What's going to happen to the art school?" I asked anxiously. I would be terribly disappointed if the classes were cancelled. "How will I explain this to the Rhodes scholarship committee at my school?"

"I can run the school myself, that is, if they let me," announced Francesca.

"Why wouldn't they let you? You've been doing it so far." I turned around again. There was the man, a respectful distance behind us.

"What's up Annie? Why do you keep turning around like that?"

"I think we're being followed," I replied. "Francesca, don't make it obvious. Stoop to tie your shoe, or drop your glove and pick it up, but look back about twenty yards down the path we're on. There's a tall guy in a blue parka and a black watch cap. See if you recognize him?"

Francesca did what I asked. "I can't tell. He's too far away. I'll look back every so often and sneak a peek. Maybe something will hit me."

In companionable silence we had reached the skating rink with its throngs of colorfully clad skaters. We watched tiny tots on two-runner skates being led around by their parents. Teenagers darted in and out of other skaters, flirting with each other. Those few semi-pro's who leaped, twirled, and spun made little islands of space as they worked through their maneuvers.

In time we became chilled. "Let's go home," I said. "I'm hungry. Want a chili-dog?"

We found a push-cart selling hot-dogs, made our purchase, and headed home, munching.

"He's there again," muttered Francesca. "Annie, you just keep walking. We don't want to let on that we've noticed him. I'm just going to walk back to the hot dog stand for some mustard. That way I can see if I recognize him." Before I could stop her, she was off. I felt for my cell, ready to call J.

I did what she said, and in a few minutes she returned. "As soon as he saw me coming toward him, he pulled his hat down and took off in the opposite direction. I didn't recognize him, but I could pick him out in a line-up."

"Try to list his features now, so you'll remember them."

Aunt J used to tell me to do that if I saw strangers around our apartment house or school. I ended up having her check up on two of the other kids' fathers. She got a big laugh out of that."

Francesca took out a piece of paper to make a quick sketch of the "blue parka" man. As we headed out of the park, and made our way cross-town, the "stranger" incident gave me an idea. "Did people come to see DiCristiani at the gallery? Is there anyone who stood out in your mind?"

"Oh, sure! Two guys in particular. They went into DC's inner sanctum. I never heard anything."

"DC. Is that what you called him?" I hadn't heard Francesca use that term for her former boss.

"Sir is what he liked to be called. I called him Mr. DiCristiani. He had this respect thing. Too bad he never figured out that it worked both ways. Do you want to know who else paid a visit?"

I nodded for her to continue.

"His son showed up a couple of times."

"I saw his picture in the paper this morning." I told her. "How old is he?"

"Early twenties, I'd say. Hot. Very hot. Slick too." She described DiCristiani's son, tall, dark, handsome, and fresh.

"What does he do? Does he work for his father?" I grew more curious, adding another character to my list. I could appreciate Francesca's colorful description despite the dangers the character might pose.

Francesca warmed to the subject and continued to describe another character for me. "He's a law student, but I got the impression that he did work for DC. I couldn't tell you what it was, though. I'm sure we'll find out. Also, I don't think they got along so well. I heard some very unfriendly exchanges between them a couple of times."

"He is good looking," I admitted, remembering his picture from the newspaper. "But he looks very tough as well."

"How would you look if your father just died?" Francesca countered.

She had a point. I thought about my own father, away on business. I always worried about plane crashes and terrorists. He traveled out of the country most of the time. A guilty pang clutched at me as I remembered that I must call him.

We reached the apartment, cold and tired. As I opened the door, I could hear Aunt J talking to someone. A deep male voice answered her unintelligible question.

"Lt. Red," I whispered to Francesca. "He's like an uncle to me. His real name is Joseph Flaherty. I just love him, and you'll see why they call him Lt. Red. He is very tall, great big shoulders, and he has the reddest hair and the most freckles I have ever seen. He's the one who's running down the leads for Aunt J. You know, checking clues."

"Yes, Annie. I watch cop shows on TV. I know the lingo."

"Hi! Lt. Red." I burst in on Aunt J and Red, dragging Francesca behind me.

Red smothered me in a bear hug. As I freed myself, he turned his gaze to Francesca, who looked a little uncomfortable.

"This is Francesca Gabrielli," I explained. "You know, the prime suspect. The one we're going to clear of this murder," I said confidently.

Lt. Red leveled a penetrating gaze on Francesca. She returned it with a steadiness that I had to admire. He nodded to her saying, "You're lucky to have these two terrors on your side, young woman."

"I know," agreed Francesca quietly.

"I need to ask you some questions, Miss Gabrielli," he said, getting down to business. "The police found two scraps of paper on the desk in DiCristiani's apartment. Evidently he kept his business records elsewhere. We're looking into that." Red dug into his pocket and pulled out his notebook. Reading glasses in place, he checked his notes.

"One was a bill from a German electronics firm, Blau Electronics. The other was a series of phone numbers, which we are tracing." He showed us the numbers. "The last few number and letter combinations are a mystery. Frankly, we don't know what they are. Does either that name or the number/letter combinations ring a bell, Miss Gabrielli? Did you ever see these when you were working with the deceased?"

Francesca looked at the list. "The first number is Frau Helriegel's home number. The others are overseas phone numbers. I can tell from the codes, but I don't know whose numbers they belong to. I remember the name, Blau Electronics, from the pieces of paper I saw when I went over to the desk to see if . . ."

Her voice cracked. "I'm sorry. It upsets me when I remember what he looked like. The other numbers and letters look like a bunch of others I've seen in his desk, but I don't know what they are."

Frowning at her, Lt. Red said, "Isn't Frau Helriegel . . ."

The phone rang, interrupting us and causing Francesca to jump an inch or two. Aunt J picked it up. After a short time, she turned to Francesca. "It's Frau Helriegel's maid. What a great phone I have here. You just mention someone's name and they call!"

"Must have gotten the number from my application at the gallery," I muttered.

She handed the phone to her, looking at Lt, Red and me with arched eyebrows. Francesca turned red and grabbed the phone.

*"Annie, I hear someone!" Francesca hissed. Startled, I
backed away from the desk where I was snooping.*

Chapter 6
PAOLO'S REQUEST

As FRANCESCA TOOK THE PHONE, I explained who the caller was to Lt. Red. I tied Frau Helriegel and Paolo into what was becoming a jig-saw puzzle of people and places.

We paused to listen to the phone conversation. "Yes, Frieda, this is Francesca. What is it?" Francesca enunciated these words loudly into the mouthpiece. During the pause, she turned to us, and mouthed the letters, D-E-A-F.

"Oh hi, Paolo," Francesca reddened even more. "What can I do for you? I've been worried about what will happen to the art classes now that Mr. DiCristiani is d . . . , uh, gone."

All eyes were on Francesca. I waited, holding my breath, hoping that Francesca would be able to continue to run the art classes. I had almost forgotten, in the excitement of the past two days, how much they meant to me.

It was so quiet we could hear the electronic buzzing of Paolo's voice on the other end. Francesca, whose knuckles were white from clutching the phone, nodded and responded to the voice we could not hear. "Yes, I would be glad to come to your home to discuss running the gallery while you're on your trip and, thank you. Thanks so much. This means so much to me."

She hung up the receiver and turned to us, relief mirrored in her face as she related to us what we already surmised. Francesca would run the gallery on a trial basis.

"Annie, can you come with me when I speak to Frau Helriegel and Paolo?" Francesca asked.

"Oh yes. I want to meet this Paolo," I agreed, winking elaborately, trying to lighten the conversation.

"Uh, don't we have school tomorrow?" Aunt J piped up.

"I don't know about anyone else, but I'm on February break and unlike my friends who are all skiing, I have art classes to attend," I replied.

"Whoops, I forgot," conceded Aunt J. "Yes, I want the two of you to stay together and check in with me. Tell me where you're going, et cetera. Remember, I trust you not to break the terms of our agreement. I am responsible for you."

She turned to Lt. Red. "Have the police already questioned Helriegel? These numbers seem to be the best lead."

Lt. Red agreed and left after admonishing Francesca to heed Aunt J's warning. "It's in your best interest to remain cooperative."

The next day we took the Number Two Train, traveling downtown and under the East River to Brooklyn and getting off at Clark St.

"Let's see." I pulled up a street map of Brooklyn Heights on my cell. Huddling together against the icy wind from the river, we found that Frau Helriegel's and Paolo's address situated them a block from the river. We headed into the breeze, walking fast to keep our blood from freezing solid.

The streets of Brooklyn Heights were narrow and lined with snow-encrusted trees, looking like Macy's Department Store windows at Christmas. The old houses, some historic, were beautifully restored and maintained. They faced the street with tall graceful windows. Stately steps led up to ornately decorated doors that seemed to speak the pride of their owners. Some had etched and beveled glass panels, others solid oak with carefully polished varnish. Brass hardware and mail boxes struggled to gleam on this dim winter day.

We came to the end of Orange Street, the full force of the wind pelting us with the first icy crystals of today's snow. We deliberately passed by the street to look at the river and the spectacular views of Manhattan Island lying before us. Tug boats and barges plied the river's treacherous currents. The skyscrapers across the way were losing their sharp details in the wavering curtain of snow.

"Francesca, is there anything at all about Frau Helriegel that makes you think that she is connected to any of DC's illegal dealings?"

"No," she concluded decisively after a short pause.

"Still and all, let's keep our eyes open when we're there. I just can't help thinking there is something under the surface. Why would she hire someone like DC?"

"You'll see when you meet them, Annie. This is a nice old lady . . ."

"And she has a very attractive grandson," I completed.

"C'mon, Annie." Francesca tugged at me.

I took another deep breath of cold air and turned to follow her back the short block to Willow St. where the buildings sheltered us from the wind.

"Why so impatient?" I teased.

"I don't want to be late. It makes a bad impression. This is a job for me and that's important. Besides, I never miss an opportunity to see Paolo, my super hero." She winked despite her grim expression.

We found the house number and climbed the steps of a lovely brownstone house with glass front doors. Heavy lace curtains maintained the privacy of those within. A fine wire for an alarm system outlined the glass in the door. Francesca pressed the door bell. After a short wait, the door opened and an elderly lady smiled at us.

"Ja?" she said in a pleasant voice.

"It's Francesca Gabrielli. I'm here to see the Helriegels about the art gallery. This is my friend, Anne Tillery."

"Ach, ja, Frauline Gabrielli! Come in, come in!"

We followed her into the house where there was delicious warmth and a more delicious aroma of coffee. She led us into a Victorian-style parlor that was inviting with its comfortable hominess.

"Please sit down," invited the woman in her heavily accented English. "I am Frieda. I vill tell them you are here. Vould you like some kafe? It's kvite cold today."

"Yes, please." We answered together as if carefully rehearsed. Frieda smiled and left. I looked around the room. Not my style. It was cluttered in the Victorian manor, but the clutter could be appreciated because of the obvious expensive nature of the various objects. There was a desk in one corner of the room, a handsome piece of woodworking, the kind with many drawers and pigeon holes. An image of another desk popped into my head, a desk I had never seen, but had imagined when Francesca had told us about finding DC, dead and slumped over that desk.

The little scraps of paper peeking out of various compartments of the desk seemed to twinkle at me, tempting, "Read me. Snoop. Read me." Could there be something there that would give us a hint about DC's murder? After all, Frau Helriegel owned the gallery which DC had used as a front for his illicit activities.

"Ach, here ve are. Zum gut fresh kafe." Frieda smiled and set down a delicate coffee service with a plate of chunky cookies that just might be chocolate chip.

"Oh, thank you," we crooned, digging into the treat.

"Frau Helriegel vill be a few moments, my dears. You vill have time to enjoy your snack." She left us.

"Francesca," I said in a loud stage whisper.

"What are you whispering for?" she said, looking annoyed.

"I'm going to snoop around in those papers on that desk over there. You sit by the door and listen. Cough, if you hear something."

"Hey, I can't get these people mad at me," she protested. I pulled out my cell, switched to the camera mode and approached the desk.

"What are you doing?" Francesca hissed. This time she was really annoyed.

"Don't worry. I'm good at this, I love to snoop. You'll see." Carefully I put my coffee cup down and went over to the desk. I looked around for some nearby object I could pretend to take interest in if I got caught. No problem here, there was enough stuff on the desk, on the wall, on the floor space around the desk to take an antique gallery curator a month to fondle and file.

One by one, I eased the papers out of their cubbies, just enough to see what was on them. Some were in German, appearing to be notes between friends.

"Annie, I hear someone!" Francesca hissed.

Startled, I backed away from the desk, intending to look as if I were gazing at a still life hanging above the desk. My foot caught on the rug. I lost my balance, bumping the coffee table. China clattered. I caught my coffee cup as it teetered on the edge of the table but my cell flew out of my hand and hit the hardwood floor with a clatter. A cookie hit the floor. Footsteps that approached the door walked on past. Our eyes locked, and we exhaled our momentary terror in unison. Francesca bent to clean up the mess. I retrieved my cell.

I went back to the desk. Just as Francesca had hissed her warning, I had seen a piece of paper with sequences of numbers and letters on it. I went back to it. I couldn't be sure, but the list looked very much like the one Lt. Red had shown us last night. This time, I positioned myself and the paper so that I could see it while appearing to gaze at the painting. If someone came in, I would merely turn, slip my cell into my pocket and smile my pleasure in the painting. *Always good to have a plan*. I congratulated myself.

I pressed the button to take a picture. The camera took one picture and the battery warning light lit up. So much for that! I started to memorize the numbers and letters in case that one picture didn't come out. I got the first four numbers in the series when I noticed Francesca rustling in her seat.

She was about to burst a blood vessel, hissing at me again, telling me to sit down. I could hear footsteps, so I pushed the paper back and moved to another painting.

A very handsome seventyish woman came through the door followed by a tall blonde gorgeous guy. "Ah, Miss Gabrielli, how are you after such a dreadful experience." Frau Helriegel extended her hand to Francesca.

"Yes, Francesca, how are you?" This from the concerned young man.

"I'm fine, thanks, Frau Helriegel, Paolo. This is my friend, Annie Tillery. She's taking the Saturday classes with us."

"How do you do." They both shook my hand, Frau Helriegel sizing me up with careful and penetrating appraisal, Paolo Helriegel with a warm smile. It was easy to see why Francesca got red ever time someone mentioned his name.

He had an open face. Vivid blue eyes peered at us through glasses that gave him an intelligent and attractive appeal. He was tall with a strong build, his handshake firm. Those hands looked like they could play the piano or handle a hammer and saw. I liked him immediately.

"We want you to take care of the Saturday art program, Francesca. And we need someone to oversee the disposition of the art acquisitions in the gallery." Frau Helriegel stated. "Do you want to take on the job?"

"Oh, yes. I've done all the work for the lessons all along, and I will learn the rest, I am sure." Francesca beamed.

As Paolo and Francesca discussed the business of running the gallery, I studied Paolo. His face read like an open book and the story line was that he liked Francesca. He expressed his concern over her discovering DiCristiani's body. He made a point to indicate his confidence and admiration regarding her skills as an artist and instructor. She responded to him with a sweetness I hadn't seen in her, tough, yes, talented, you bet, scared too. But this sweet side was new. I liked it.

Paolo explained that he and his grandmother needed to go to Germany on business and then enumerated what they expected of her, as well as a salary arrangement.

Francesca looked anxiously at Frau Helriegel.

"You know that I am a suspect in Mr. DiCristiani's murder, don't you?" It must have been hard for Francesca to bring that up on the brink of her best piece of luck yet.

"Why, because you had the misfortune to find the body? We were becoming aware of his, how do you say it, shady nature. His death saves me the trouble of trying to fire him," Frau Helriegel confirmed. Her coldness raised the hairs on my neck, even if I had to agree with her analysis of the man. I wondered if this refined lady could kill a man.

Francesca gazed at them, unable to find her voice. "Thank you. I'm so grateful for the opportunity. I'm just having a hard time believing my luck." Francesca's voice cracked a little as she squeezed back her tears.

With a quick change of gears, Frau Helriegel added, "I love the gallery, and especially the opportunity it gives me to reach out to young talent." She said this with undisguised emotion, and I couldn't help feeling this was her special message to me.

I smiled my most polite smile, feeling a tinge of guilt for snooping. But the snoop in me won out in the end, and I concentrated on remembering the list I had discovered.

Francesca would fill me in on whatever else happened as a result of our visit.

At last, the business arrangements taken care of, Paolo made arrangements to have lunch with Francesca the next day to clarify what her responsibilities would be. At least that's what he gave as an excuse for a lunch date. I think Paolo had a thing for Francesca and I knew she wasn't minding it a bit.

We left the house. I walked down the stately steps. Francesca was walking on air. As soon as we were around the corner, I wrote down what I had seen on that list, as best as I could remember, in a tiny notebook I carried in my pocket.

"Wow! How things can change," my companion exclaimed, paying no attention to me at all. "Yesterday, I was worried about the death penalty. Today I have a dream job and a dream date."

"Aren't you afraid it's a lot to handle?" I asked.

Her face clouded over. "Don't you believe in romance, Annie?" she protested. "This would be overwhelming, if I didn't believe in love and happy endings." She turned to see my reaction.

"Yeah, I do. My romantic interest and I were supposed to be skiing in Vermont this week, but he's in the middle of a research project he can't leave."

"Well, then you understand. I really like him, Annie. He's as nice as my brothers, and such a contrast to DiCristiani and his sleazy son Mark."

"Yup, He is nice, very sexy too. And, those blue eyes, Mmmmm"

"Who's this research guy?" Francesca asked.

"Tyler Egan. I met him on Fire Island last summer. He's really nice too. We text and email and see each other on breaks. He stayed with Aunt J and me for Christmas break."

"I want to hear more, but I've got to get back to the gallery. What was that you were writing?"

"I saw a list of number and letters while I was snooping and I had to memorize as many as I could before they came in. My cell camera ran out of juice at just the critical moment. I wonder if there's a connection between the list they found on DC's desk and the ones I just found."

"You're not the only one who can snoop," Francesca confided, a triumphant look on her face. I looked at her, wondering what she had up her sleeve.

"Now that I'm in charge of taking care of the gallery's inventory, I have, rather we have, the freedom to go through DC's desk at the gallery."

"Let's do it," I agreed. We rode the subway back across the river to downtown Manhattan in silence, each of us wondering what DC's desk might hold.

Chapter 7
THE CRIME SCENE

WE WENT THROUGH THE DESK, one drawer at a time, carefully emptying the contents onto a tabletop, sorting it, returning it. We even checked the drawer frame and the bottom of each drawer. We looked for secret compartments, false bottoms. All that came up were a few bills from the ever-popular Blau Electronics, and a small black address book. The detectives in charge of the investigation had already impounded DiCristiani's computer and tax records, but they hadn't found anything of interest in this part of the office. It didn't surprise me. This desk looked like just another piece of antique furniture in this beautiful house. If this office were still part of a crime scene, it would've been off-limits to the public, and to us as well.

"What's this?" A house-cleaning party? Couldn't even wait for the body to get cold, huh?"

I hate getting caught. Francesca, on the other hand, seemed to have more experience at it, because she regained her composure quickly.

"Annie, this is Mark DiCristiani," she said introducing us.

He gave me the once over, eyes lingering over my face and body for a little too long to be flattering. He made me uncomfortable.

Mark DiCristiani was even more handsome in person, and yes, not only tall, dark and handsome, but fresh. He had a slim gold chain over his gray turtle neck, a bulky gold wristwatch that looked like it could calculate the movements of the planets, and a large square gold ring.

Francesca interrupted my appraisal. "Frau Helriegel asked me to take care of the gallery until she decides what to do about replacing your father. I'm looking through the papers and organizing things."

Looking him square in the eye, her smile not much of a bluff for the firmness in her voice, she said, "I'm looking for the bills for the paintings of mine that he sold. You know, the copies?" She was testing the waters here, reaching to see what he would say. She knew there were no bills.

"I don't know anything about my dad's paperwork. But I was thinking of asking you to do similar kinds of works for me. I have the same contacts, and I think I should carry on some of his business ventures."

I could see red climbing up Francesca's neck as she loaded her verbal guns for the response. I kicked her, hoping she would catch on to what a great opportunity this was to have Mark say something interesting. Lucky, we were both behind the desk where he couldn't see my foot hit her shin.

"Uh, yeah, we'll talk, Mark," she responded, getting control. Thankfully, she did catch on.

"Nice ring, Mark," I ventured to break the tension.

"Yeah," he said admiring the ring on a hand that was slim with long fingers and fine dark hair. "It's sort of a graduation ring. I belong to a club, and when you prove your, uh, manhood, you get the ring." He grinned that surly smile that turned his handsome face ugly. I blushed.

Attempting to change the subject, Francesca asked, "When do you plan on removing your father's belongings from the gallery?"

"I wouldn't count on that happening too soon. I've got good lawyers. We may get the gallery impounded."

I snorted and quickly tried to cover it with a cough. Mark, the perfect gentleman, turned and loomed over me, menacing me with a raised hand. That did it.

"Just try it! As they say, 'Make my day!' My aunt will have your butt in jail so fast, it'll take your crack lawyers a week to realize what happened."

He backed up, raising both hands in a conciliatory gesture.

"Well, I'll be back soon, and I'm glad to see that you have an assistant, Miss, Gabrielli. I'll be looking for you, Annie. I really look forward to that." He left with a leer and a wink.

"Like father, like son," Francesca muttered. "I am very afraid of him. Let's find what we can here and get out."

"He thinks he's slick, I guess," I replied, pulling out the last drawer. I dumped out the contents, turning it upside down. There it was! Taped to the bottom of the drawer was a list of number and letters.

"Go get the number/letter things you copied from Frau Helriegel's desk!" Francesca's voice was hushed, but urgent.

I knew what I would find. I still remembered two of the combinations I had memorized earlier today. I plucked my list from my coat pocket. Laying them side by side, we stared at the two sets. All the ones I had managed to remember had mates on the list we had just removed from the drawer.

"We have to take this to Aunt J and Lt. Red. These numbers keep showing up. It can't be a coincidence."

Francesca nodded, "If we find out what these mean, or who they belong to, it could lead us to the murderer."

We stared at the two lists for another moment or two. Finally, Francesca slumped into a chair, rubbing her neck. "Tension", she breathed. "I'm so tired."

She yawned, and contagious as they are, I soon was joining her. "It's late. Lets' clean up and go home." I pocketed the list.

The subway ride back uptown was almost relaxing. Francesca and I rode in silence, weary, reeling from the enormity of the events of the last couple of days, as they sunk into our brains. Aunt J was home when we got to the apartment. Good smells came from the kitchen, reminding us that our last meal was two chocolate chip cookies in Brooklyn Heights.

"Hey guys! What's up?" J put a platter of pasta with a rich meat sauce down on the dining room table between a bowl of salad and a basket of bread. The dining room was warm and smelled lusciously of garlic.

"Just tired and hungry."

"Then let's eat and you can tell me about your day," J said, gesturing toward the table. "But wash up. The pasta's very hot."

I loved my Aunt J. She had a demanding job, but she still seemed to find time to make a home for us. It made me happy to come home to our apartment and feel its warmth and her love.

We did as we were told and returned to the table. The food worked its magic and conversation grew livelier with our account of the day.

"I want to see those lists," said Aunt J, her brow puckering. "Lt. Red is working on the one from DiCristiani's apartment." She looked at Francesca and me. "Francesca, you will have to go down to headquarters tomorrow. They want hair and blood samples from you."

"What does that mean?" Francesca put her fork down, swallowed hard and looked up at my aunt, almost choking on her pasta.

"It means that they have collected some physical evidence at the crime scene and they want to see if any of it is a match to you."

"I've been in that apartment before. I could have left evidence at some previous visit," Francesca protested.

"I thought you only went into the foyer?" Aunt J gave Francesca a piercing look.

Francesca looked down at her plate. "Yeah, that's right," was all she could reply. My curiosity piqued.

"I'll take you downtown with me. It'll only take a few minutes. Francesca, if you're innocent, you have nothing to worry about." Aunt J reached out and gave Francesca's hand a reassuring squeeze.

The next morning I went to the gallery to work on my sketch from the first lesson. Francesca would come to the gallery after she was finished downtown. On the way I had wondered about Francesca's evasiveness at dinner last night and promised myself that I would try to find out what it meant.

My optimism was returning. The lessons would continue. Clues seemed to be turning up. I felt confident that Francesca would be cleared. I set to work on the sketch. Time passed quickly as I worked on the details of the old Asian man's face.

"It's time to give away secrets of the trade, I see."

Startled, I dropped my pencil. I turned to see Francesca storing her coat in the closet. "How'd it go?"

"Okay," Francesca muttered frowning at my drawing. "Bones! You have to visualize the bones. That's the key to making the face have real depth."

It was my turn to frown. "How do you visualize the bones in the face?"

"You go out and buy *Gray's Anatomy* and you study the bones. And you study how the muscles are attached to the bones."

"How do I put that down on paper?"

"Work with values, rather than lines, shades of gray, as they say. I'm a poet and don't even know it."

Francesca looked at me, studying my face intensely for a moment.

"I'll show you what I mean," she said picking up the sketch pad and pencil. "Okay. What I'm seeing first is the general shape of your face. It's basically oval, and the proportions are regular. Your jaw line is a little fuller than the classic oval. See? I'm visualizing your jaw bone."

I watched as she lightly sketched the shape of my face.

"Now, I have to try to picture the bones that give your skin its contours. This is where the shading comes in. Your jaw is offset by the fact that your eyes are set wide. If you had close-set eyes, your face would look square. Also, your cheek bones are high so there are nice hollows running in a line from ear to mouth. That gives your face interest." She started to shade areas of the face she had outlined on the pad.

"Hmmm. I never noticed your teeth, but I know they're even, no overbite or anything. I can tell that from your lips, which form the classic mouth. Your nose is average, so I'm giving you the typical Caucasoid nasal bone, and then just the right amount of flare."

"It doesn't look a lot like me, yet there is something familiar," I said, appraising her work.

"The eyes will do it," she explained. "Yours are not deeply set, but you've got nice brow ridges. That's what makes for good eyebrows."

As she filled in the eyes, brows and hair, I looked on in admiration.

"Wow! It is me."

"I hope so," she replied. "If I can't do a sketch that looks like you, I might as well hang it up. What is harder to do is to capture an expression that is typically you. You have a serious face, but a great smile when you decide to use it. And black-and-white doesn't suit you. The gray-green eyes and honey hair are a distinct advantage to your looks. But as you can see, I had to visualize the bones first to get the face. It's the same for bodies, especially hands and feet. You are tall. That helps people to notice your face, since you are above the crowd. And Annie, I mean it. Above the crowd." Francesca's voice cracked and we hugged as I blushed.

"Really, Francesca, how did it go?" I said returning to the subject. I turned to see her staring out the window, shoulders stiff with tension.

"I'm scared, Annie. I had the motive. I had the opportunity. Now, I'm afraid they'll find something that I left in the apartment to link me to the murder scene."

"They have to prove that you're guilty. You don't have to prove that you're innocent. If they find something of yours in the apartment, you'll have to tell them about being there. In the apartment, I mean." This last part I said slowly, and pointedly, seeing my opportunity to get to the bottom of Francesca's evasiveness last night.

She looked at me. "Yes. I was in the apartment. Only once, though. He tried to hit on me. We had quite a struggle. I kicked him in the groin and ran. That's part of why he hated me."

"Why didn't you tell us about that?"

"Because the whole thing is so sleazy, I wanted it buried in the past," she sighed.

I couldn't bring myself to ask her if she'd killed DiCristiani. But, it nagged at me. My gut said she didn't do it. The circumstances of the situation were beginning to stack up against her, though.

I haven't seen Francesca so down. Trying to brighten her day, I asked about the lunch with Paolo scheduled for today.

"It's off," she replied in the same dejected tone. "They had to take an earlier flight."

"Oh, I'm sorry," *Really sorry!* I thought. "Let's spend our energy thinking how we can find out who really did this."

Francesca nodded, and walked back to my sketch. "Your proportions are good," she proclaimed, trying to ease the discomfort we were both feeling.

"So is my judgment," I answered her. "Let's talk about the crime scene, Francesca. Maybe we can come up with something. You know, if you can remember exactly what you did, we might figure out what you left there, if anything."

Francesca poured coffee from the Mr. Coffee. I put down my sketch pad, grabbed a legal pad and joined her at the desk. "Francesca. Let's sit down, and go over the crime scene, step by step. Do you feel calm enough to do that? Tell me everything that happened from the time you set eyes on the apartment house. There must be something that you'll remember that would help prove your innocence. I'll write it all down, and we'll give it to Aunt J. Things that don't seem important to us, she might find significant."

Francesca sat down with her coffee mug, rubbing her brow with thumb and index finger. "I'm trying to visualize the apartment house when I walked up to it that day."

"Good. Take your time. I'll try not to interrupt, but I'll write down everything you say."

"The worst part of making those pickups was going up the back stairs. He never wanted me to take the elevator."

"Why?"

"He said he didn't want anyone at his residence observing any of his business dealings or transactions. He said his neighbors wouldn't like it. Now, I know that he just didn't want any visible connection with me. In case the fakes were discovered, he would blame the whole thing on me. Anyway, I started up the back stairs."

"You never saw anyone? Anyone you could recognize?"

"Hang on, I'm getting there. As I was going up, this guy was coming down, whistling. I can't tell you what he looked like. He had a hat like the ones they used to wear in those old gangster movies. You know, pulled low over his face. He also had a big overcoat with the collar turned up. I didn't think anything of it at the time."

"Can you describe anything else about him?" I said, pen poised.

Francesca squeezed her eyes shut. "He was a big man, over six feet, fair skinned. I noticed his hand on the banister as I passed. The hair on the back of it was blond."

"You saw his hand? Did you see a ring, a watch, a scar?"

"Yes! I didn't think of it before. There was a ring. Gold. I think there was an initial on it."

"What letter, Francesca. Think!"

"One with all straight lines, F E I, I'm not sure. Maybe he had nothing to do with DiCristiani."

"Someone murdered him. You didn't. That someone had to enter and leave because the crime scene unit didn't find a murderer in the closet. So, go on, let's see what else you can remember."

This was getting exciting! Finally, another lead. I wondered how Aunt J could use this.

"When I got to the apartment, everything seemed the same as always." Francesca picked up the thread of her account. "The door was unlocked. I went in. The foyer looked like it usually did, except there was no package for me in the basket. I was a little surprised that the door was unlocked. But, I figured that's the way it always was."

"What do you mean?"

"That the outer door was always open. It could be for a variety of reasons. What really surprised me was that the inside door was open. That never happened before. I went to see him. So, I knocked, rang the bell and waited. Nothing."

"Did you hear anything?

"N . . . Wait a minute! I forgot about it until now. It was so awful, finding him like that, Annie. There was so much blood."

"What did you hear?" I prompted, trying to move her away from the horror of her memory.

"Remember? I told Aunt J about this when you met me at the police station. I heard that door close, somewhere in the back of the apartment. But that's all. No footsteps. Like the wind shut a door, or a ghost." She shivered. "Maybe DiCristiani's ghost was leaving the apartment." She looked at me. I rolled my eyes, but shivered too, thinking about a ghost I met last summer.

"Or maybe it was the killer. Are you sure you didn't hear anything else? Or see, or smell anything different."

"It smelled like fire crackers when I got there. Of course, that had to be from the gunshots. I forgot about that."

"Good. You're remembering more stuff. Let's hope you'll remember something that will lead us to the real killer."

Francesca went over to one of the drafting tables and began to sketch with charcoal. "I'm an artist. I should be able to draw the guy on the stairs."

"Draw what your first impression was. That will help you to remember the rest, to fill in the details. That's how the police artists work when they sketch a suspect from an eye-witness account."

As she sketched, I fleshed out my notes on what she had told me so far.

"That's all I can do for now. I'll go back to it," she announced after a few minutes had gone by. I looked at the mystery figure. Francesca had caught the man's rapid motion, and clouded features, conveying the idea that he was trying to escape notice. I admired her talent. The only part of the sketch that was detailed was his hand.

"Okay. What did you do when you went into the apartment? Better still, can you recall the layout of the apartment? We can make a sketch of the crime scene."

Francesca set to work, and soon produced a reasonable floor plan for the apartment's entry-way, foyer and living room. "Here's the desk where his body was."

"So then, you couldn't see him if you just looked in the door? Did you go right over to him?"

"Yes. I shook him. The rug was soaked with blood. He was lying in a pool of it. As soon as I realized what the blood meant, I dropped his arm and backed away. The next thing I knew the super came in, and started shaking me. I guess I was screaming a lot. You know the rest of the story."

"Do you remember seeing anything on the desk or in the room that the murderer may have left?"

"There were the two papers on the desk. You already know about them. One was the bill. I can remember the name Blau. The other was that list of numbers. I can't explain how I remember them so well. Maybe trauma brands the memory with what you are seeing at that time into your brain. But, I don't remember any other things."

"The police took blood and hair samples from you this morning because they found something in the room that didn't match up to DiCristiani. His hair and blood should be there. He lives there. I guess what I'm asking you to recall is an item of clothing, maybe other spots of blood on the carpet or on the door knob."

"I remember DiCristiani's hands. Actually, the image of what he looked like is something that flashes into my head from time to time, all day long, and in my dreams." She shook herself as if to rid herself of that distasteful image. "There was something in his hand, something dark. It might just have been blood, but I do remember being drawn to his hand. I would have looked into it, but then I saw the side of his head in the puddle of blood. That's when I freaked."

"DiCristiani might have grabbed the murderer. I bet that's what they found."

"What if they found something of mine that I left before?"

"You're going to have to tell them everything," I said this in my most convincing voice. I believed that there was a good chance that Francesca had left evidence during her previous visits.

Francesca nodded, and then hung her head, turning away, but not fast enough to hide her tears from me. She picked up the sketch of the mystery man. "Maybe this guy is the murderer," she sighed in a low voice.

I went over to her and hugged her. She worked on the charcoal sketch, deciding to switch to pencil. I filled in the details of my drawing of DiCristiani's apartment. We both jumped as the phone rang.

Francesca reached for it. "Hello, Paolo," It was as if someone turned a light on inside of her. The gray gloom of our conversation was banished by her warm blush. "Are you at the airport."

She listened for a moment then switched to the speaker phone. His voice echoed out in a tinny tone, "There is a package for you in Brooklyn Heights. It contains a list of possible art works that you may want to procure for the gallery. The names of the owners and directions for taking care of the paper work for sale of art pieces are all there with the documents I was supposed to give you at lunch. You must use your judgment to get the best pieces."

"We'll pick it up when we leave here," Francesca replied, sounding confident.

"Give our best to Max and Frieda," Paolo urged. "And how are you, Francesca?"

"I'm scared, Paolo. I had to give my blood and hair samples at police headquarters today."

"This can only help to clear you, Francesca. I know it will all work out. Paolo's sincerity rang through the speaker phone. "I wish I was there to support you. We will be back as soon as possible. Next time, we will have a lunch date, no business to take care of. That's a promise." It was hard to ignore the warmth in his voice.

"Annie is helping me to remember everything I can about the crime scene. I don't know what I would have done without her and her Aunt J." She winked at me, rubbing away tears with the sleeve of her sweatshirt.

"She's a very promising artist. You should give her a part-time job," she pushed.

"We'll think about that. I must go now. I'll check in with you soon. If you need us, Max and Frieda have our number."

"Good-bye, Paolo," I called out. The connection was broken. Francesca hung up.

"He likes you, Francesca," I said quietly. "You're going to be okay. You have a knight in shining armor." She smiled, still flushed.

I was grateful for Paolo's call. Francesca had needed the boost. I had a brief thought of my knight in shining armor in Vermont.

"We about done here?" I asked, shaking away the daydream.

"Let me take these ledgers home with me," Francesca responded. "I can get a feel for what goes on with the business end of the gallery if I take a good look at them."

We locked up and left. It was another frigid afternoon, but no snow. The downtown train to Brooklyn was crowded, and the walk to Willow St. was tortuous to our tired bodies. At first, I paid no attention to the noises of the city, but as we approached the river, the sound of fire sirens grew loud. "Must be nearby," I speculated.

We rounded the last corner, only to behold the glare and flashing of the fire truck lights.

"Gee, it's on this block," said Francesca.

Suddenly, gripped by the same fear, we started to run toward the familiar brownstone. Our premonition exploded into reality in front of us as we saw Frau Helriegel's brownstone being doused by New York's bravest, black smoke billowing up into the gray sky. Two EMT's emerged from the front door with a stretcher. Francesca and I could only stare.

Chapter 8
OUT OF THE ASHES

THE FIRST STRETCHER WAS FOLLOWED by a second. It took a minute to realize that this wasn't an episode of some TV show. Those were real people who were being carried out, oxygen masks on their faces, IV bags being held by the EMT's. At least they were alive.

"That must be Max and Frieda," Francesca croaked, her hand shaking as she grasped mine. "Let's go tell them we're here." We tried to run to the ambulance but were grabbed by a policeman who was in the process of stretching yellow crime-scene tape around the area.

The beautiful brownstone was a mess. The beveled glass etched with flowers that made the door so charming was a sprinkling of glass shards scattered all over the front steps. Smoke belched out of the tall bay windows, also smashed by the firemen's axes, blackening the bricks above. Filthy water, streaming from the front entrance floor was invading the little piles of pristine snow, turning them sooty. The blare of emergency vehicles hurt my ears, making conversation almost impossible.

"We're employees of the owner," cried Francesca. "The owners are on their way to Germany. Those two people are the housekeepers. Can we please go to them? They might feel better if they could see a familiar face," she pleaded.

"Can I have some ID?" the sergeant demanded.

"I'm Anne Tillery." I offered him my school identification card. He took it, looking at me curiously. Francesca produced her driver's license.

"What made you show up here just at this very moment?" the policeman demanded squinting at our ID.

Francesca explained in a careful polite voice that she worked for the owner of the house at the owner's art gallery in Soho, and that she was here to pick up a package of materials she needed to run the gallery in the owner's absence. I noticed that she failed to mention anything about the DiCristiani connection.

"I don't suppose I could go in, now that the fire is out, and look for my package," Francesca wheedled. The smoke had indeed, stopped pouring out of the house.

"No, young lady, I don't care who or what you are. There'll be an investigation here. I'll talk to the detective in charge about your going to the hospital with the two casualties. Wait here!" Gesturing to a spot on the sidewalk, he yelled, "Officer Blanco, keep an eye on these two till I get back." Off he went, leaving us under the suspicious surveillance of Office Blanco.

"I can't help but feel that this is not a coincidence," I muttered to Francesca. She just stood there, looking stunned, eyes taking in the shocking scene.

A dapper man of about fifty, dressed in a camel-colored top coat and fashionable felt hat, came over to us. "I'm Detective Frank McDonnell with N.Y.P.D." He nodded at me. "Miss Tiller, I have the pleasure of knowing your aunt." He turned to Francesca. "Miss Gabrielli," he smiled without much warmth. "You do have a knack for turning up at some of the city's trouble spots, young lady."

Francesca stuck out her small chin. "I'm an employee of the owners of this house. I was here on business."

"That was your excuse the last time, I believe. Wasn't it?" His tone was sarcastic. He turned to me, dismissing whatever reply Francesca was going to make.

"She's been with either my aunt or me since DiCristiani's murder, Detective McDonnell." I came to Francesca's defense, smiling sweetly. *So keep your sarcastic crap to yourself*, I thought to myself, attempting to take some command of the situation.

"We'd like to accompany Max and Frieda to the hospital," Francesca spoke up again, explaining how their employer was in Germany and that the two elderly people would find comfort in a familiar face. "I have a phone number where she can be reached in-flight, and one for her office in Germany, if you'd like to check out my story," she offered.

"She'll have to be officially notified about the fire and casualties anyway," McDonnell stated in a bored tone. "Wait here. I'm going to check out your story with Tillery."

"That's Detective Tillery, you oaf," I muttered under my breath.

"What was that, Miss Tillery?"

"I said what a good idea, sir." Again, I gave him my sweetest smile, stomach turning at his attitude.

He turned to go. Francesca slumped against the wall as we rolled our eyes at Detective McDonnell's helpful manner.

"I want to get to a phone and contact Frau Helriegel and Paolo before they do," Francesca confided, pointing in the direction of one of the patrol cars.

"I don't think there's a chance of that right now."

"Can I use your cell?" Francesca asked.

"I don't have an international chip in it," I replied.

Mr. Obnoxious, aka McDonnell, returned, explaining that we could go to the hospital and meet Max and Frieda there. We could not go with them in the ambulance.

"Look, let's get to a phone. You try your contact numbers and see what the Frau wants to do, and I'll call Aunt J on my cell. Detective McDonnell doesn't have her cell phone number, or her beeper."

"You want me to call Germany from a pay phone?" she stared at me as if I had just announced that I was about to grow male body parts.

"Sorry! Not thinking!" I said. "Let me call Aunt J first, and you can give her the number."

We trotted back to the subway station as I made the call to my aunt.

"Let's get the train. We can talk on the way," I said, steering Francesca towards the turnstile.

"What did your aunt say when you told her what happened?"

"I can't repeat some of it, but the bottom line is that she was not happy with Detective McDonnell. She's meeting us at the hospital."

We arrived at New York Presbyterian Hospital, and found our way to the emergency room. I let out a sigh of relief as I caught sight of Aunt J at the nurses' station. Lt. Red was there also.

"Did you find out how bad they are?" Francesca panted, rushing up to Aunt J and Lt. Red.

"Not serious," replied Lt. Red. "Minor smoke inhalation, they are mostly scared. And, or course, their age is a factor."

Aunt J turned from the nurses' station. "Well, you two never have a dull moment, do you?" She smiled, shaking her head. "Why were you there in the first place?"

Francesca explained the phone call from Paolo and the package.

"You know that there's an arson investigation in progress," Aunt J explained.

"From the preliminary findings, it looks very suspicious. This gets curiouser and curiouser, as the little girl with the rabbit used to say."

The nurse gestured to us. "You can go in now," she explained, pointing us in the right direction.

We filed into a room where both Max and Frieda were sitting in hospital recliners. Both were hooked up to IV's. Both had an oxygen line taped to their nostrils. Frieda looked frightened until she saw Francesca and me.

"Ach! Got sie dank! Someone ve know!" Aunt J and Red introduced themselves, and asked if they felt up to being questioned about the fire.

"Ja, ja. Ve must get to the bottom of dis. Our Frau vill be most upset," Frieda said, trembling.

"Now, now, Frieda. Your heart. Calm yourself. Ve are lucky to be alive," assured Max, patting his beloved wife's hand.

"Yes, please, both of you. You must remain calm, and try to remember every detail that could give us information about how the fire started, and if it is arson, who started it." Lt. Red's manner had the desired effect on the housekeepers. Aunt J began her interrogation asking Max and Frieda that first most obvious question about having seen strangers near the house or in the neighborhood. The only thing Max could remember was an odd phone call before the fire. The caller warned them to get out of the house to avoid a grave danger. Since they are not easily frightened, they checked the house anyway. A few moments later they heard a loud bang in the basement. That's when the house filled with smoke making it impossible to see into the basement to find the source of the noise. Frieda explained that she called the Fire Department.

"Ja, ve could see the flames coming up de stairs by den," added Max.

"Ve started to go to de door. Dat is ven Max collapsed just inside de door, but de firemen came den to save us," she finished.

"You must try to remember every single detail about the last few days. Anything that struck you as out of the ordinary might be important," Lt Red urged, repeating his request.

I listened carefully, wondering what information they could give that would help.

"De only ting I can remember dat vas different vas dat the terrible noises from de building next door had stopped," Max offered.

Aunt J and Lt. Red exchanged glances. "What awful noises?" they asked in unison.

Max explained that there was a construction project in the house next door.

Frieda started to cry. "What will our Frau do, she loved dat house. Ve have let her down," she sobbed.

"No. You have been the victims of a crime. You must rest now. I'm sure your employer will need your help in getting her house back to order." Aunt J patted them both reassuringly.

Francesca grasped Frieda's hand and assured both of them that the Frau and Paolo were most concerned about their welfare.

"I want you to do me a big favor, Mr. and Mrs. Schmidt." Lt Red said this in his most serious and confidential tone. "Think about all the things that happened in the last few days. Write down anything that you think might be important. We'll check with you tomorrow."

The nurse came in, and we left. Aunt J's Camry was outside, and we headed for the apartment. Lt. Red explained that he wanted to get our story for the record.

Francesca and I were both asleep within seconds after snuggling up in the warm car. Aunt J nudged us, and we struggled out of our little nap. The elevator ride to our floor did little to wake us.

"I'll make coffee. I'm afraid you girls will have to make it for a couple of more hours," she announced. Fifteen minutes later, we all sat down. The coffee and what Lt. Red had to say had me wide awake in a minute.

"What I have to say stays right in this room, girls." He said this with such a stern look that we both nodded solemnly. How easily he slid into his serious Law-and-Order mask and out of his jovial Lt. Red one. "I'm only going to tell you the results of my investigation, because I think that Francesca might be able to shed light on it in some way. You've seen and heard things while working in the gallery. You may be able to help."

I wondered whether that last statement was his real motive or was he trying to set a trap for Francesca.

Francesca frowned and nodded slowly, "I'll try."

Lt. Red filled us in on what his efforts had uncovered so far. He gave us a brief sketch of Frau Helriegel, telling us that she was completely legit, and very wealthy. Her money came from her husband's electronics business. DiCristiani, on the other hand, had some of the shadiest and most unsavory contacts and associates that are known to the N.Y.P.D. On the surface, his company, *DiCristiani Enterprises International,* is legitimate. But it's believed that it is a front for drug smuggling, money laundering and fencing stolen jewelry and art pieces. Nothing has ever stuck from any investigation and he has no rap sheet.

He continued, "Now, why does Frau Helriegel hire such a shady guy to run a gallery for her?" The icing on the cake is that when we ran the check on his business holdings, we find that he owns the brownstone next to Frau Helriegel's. He bought it a year ago." Red finished his summary, dropping this surprise package in our laps.

Francesca and I looked at each other. Lt. Red went on, "Now, we have this fire, of suspicious nature. By the way, it is arson. I'm just waiting for the official word."

"How can you know its arson?" I asked.

Red gave us the amateur version of pyromania 101. Launching into his subject, pardon the pun, he explained how arsonists leave a signature, like most career criminals. They fall into four categories; nuts, guys looking for insurance or to cover another crime and the professionals." Lt. Red warmed to the subject. Professionals did this job. They have several ways of starting a fire. The sloppy ones use accelerants like gasoline. The more sophisticated ones start the process with a small explosion or an electrical device.

"How do you hide a small explosion?" Francesca asked dubiously.

As always I admired Lt. Red's knowledge of so many areas of forensic science. He responded to Francesca's question, telling her that small battery operated incendiary devices called fuses were placed near the furnace. They would be almost totally burned because they were near the source of the fire they had started in the first place. Since some of the metal pieces would not be destroyed, this is how arson experts could determine that the fire was arson, and who did it. The "fuse" was the signature of the arsonist, and could lead the investigation to an individual arsonist.

"Why is this person out there still doing it if you know who he is?" I demanded.

"Because we know him or her by the other cases they've done, not by a name," Lt. Red replied. "When we do get him, he'll never make it out of prison."

"There do seem to be too many strange links between Frau Helriegel and DiCristiani," I said.

"And too many bizarre occurrences," added Francesca.

"Bizarre occurrence is a nice way of putting murder and arson," Aunt J observed with a wry snort.

"The key seems to be Frau Helriegel," I said, suddenly thinking of the list of letters and numbers. "Lt Red, did you get anywhere with the list from DiCristiani's office." That might give us the link we needed.

"I can't believe the Frau has anything to do with DiCristiani's underworld activities," Francesca protested. "He must have conned her somehow. You don't know how slick and charming he can be." Francesca seemed to be smarting from her memories of her own experiences with DiCristiani.

"Remember though," I countered, "she did say she was beginning to doubt his honesty."

"I have found a few things out regarding that list," Red answered. "Blau Electronics is owned by one Horst Blau. He is another interesting character who's tied up with both DiCristiani and the Frau. Horst is Paolo Helriegel's godfather. Horst and the Frau know each other from the old country. He is extremely wealthy also, as a result of his family's electronics business. Another coincidence?"

"We found a lot of mail from Blau Electronics when we went through DiCristiani's desk at the gallery," I offered candidly.

"My little Agatha Christie," Aunt J said grinning unconvincingly.

Francesca turned red. "How can I run the business unless I know what's been going on?" She fumbled for an explanation for our search.

"We searched his desk," I owned up. "We were looking for anything that might lead us to his murderer. Francesca has a real interest in that, don't you think?"

"Did you find anything?" Aunt J prodded.

"As a matter of fact, look at this list." I produced our find and Lt. Red took it with a low whistle.

"Whadaya know," he breathed.

"Not so surprising," I observed. "It's like the one found near his body. And the one I memorized from Frau Helriegel's house. What's happening with the list from the crime scene?"

"The list is a puzzle," Red declared. "I've traced some of them, but there is one set that I can't crack. Our computer people are looking at them. They do have other cases to work on. Still I can't help feeling that the list is the key that will tell us how Frau Helriegel and DiCristiani have become connected." Red looked pensively down at his notes.

"What else did you find in the office?" Aunt J asked.

"Just the list and the Blau Electronics bills. The rest seemed pretty regular," I replied.

"When will I know about the results of my blood and hair test?" Francesca looked up at Red and Aunt J with a worried face.

"We'll know tomorrow, Francesca," Aunt J answered.

"What did they find at DiCristiani's place that they need a match for?" I asked.

"Some blood that was not DiCristiani's type and hairs on his jacket," Aunt J replied simply. "Francesca, if there's no match between your blood and the crime scene blood, you're in the clear. If there is, you are in serious trouble."

Chapter 9

FRANCESCA'S MASTERPIECE

"WAKE UP. HEY! IT'S OKAY."

Someone has come to save me from the fire. I can't run. Something is holding my legs. I struggled to free myself. Opening my eyes, Francesca was sitting at the edge of the bed, shaking me. I couldn't move my legs because she was on top of the covers.

"You okay?" She peered at me.

"Yeah. Oh, bad, bad dream. I was in the brownstone fire. I was trying to save a painting that was in the basement, but DiCristiani locked the door."

"I hope the painting that you were trying to save was worth it," Francesca offered.

"It was the one that I kept staring at while I was snooping in Frau Helriegel's desk. Let me out of bed. Where were you going?" I asked, noticing her coat.

"I'm going to go to the gallery. Paolo said he would send me a duplicate list to the one we were supposed to pick up at the house in Brooklyn. I wanted to get started on contacting some of the leads. The secretary comes in today, and I need her help."

"Can't you wait for me?"

"Can you hurry?"

"Fifteen minutes," I replied. "Have another cup of coffee."

Twenty minutes later, as I grabbed a quick drink of OJ, I saw Aunt J's note, "Call me at HQ at two for test results."

"Did you see Aunt J's note?" I called to Francesca.

"Yup. That's another reason to get busy. If I sit around waiting for those results, I'll lose my mind," Francesca declared in a glum voice.

We arrived at the gallery. By agreement, while she sorted the mail, I set the conservatory up for the next art class. It required moving everything around, the easels, the model's platform and the supply table. I had an idea for improving the lighting on the model. As I was working up a sweat, the phone rang.

"Frau Helriegel!" I heard Francesca's voice from the office. "How are you? Are you and Paolo on your way home?" Francesca clutched the phone tightly. Reaching for the button for speaker phone, she signaled me to be quiet.

I listened as Francesca gave Frau Helriegel an update on Max and Frieda's condition. She also gave necessary details about the fire and the condition of the house.

"The police must be searching the basement very thoroughly." It was hard to miss the anxiety in Frau Helriegel's voice, barely disguised by the speaker phone.

"I guess so. That would seem logical." Francesca shot me a confused glance.

"I—I'm trying to assess the damages. I want to be able to calculate how long before we can live in our home," she added nervously. "Tell Max and Frieda that I will be home in the morning. I must go now." She hung up.

"What do you make of that?" I asked.

"She seemed more interested in the condition of the basement than in Max and Frieda. Go figure." Francesca sighed. "I wanted to get some work done here today."

"Let's visit Max and Frieda today. I have an idea. Visiting hours are not until two," I offered. "We can get plenty of work done before then. We can make the most of our visit. We could tactfully ease into a discussion of the basement. Maybe they know what's so special down there. Maybe they know what has Frau Helriegel in such a fit."

"Two is when we have to call your aunt." Francesca sounded so scared that I looked at her, trying to think how I could encourage her or be optimistic.

"We'll call before we leave here. Okay?"

We spent the next few hours working. I finished my furniture moving. The secretary came in at noon, and Francesca had a list of bills and correspondence for her to take care of. The desk in DiCristiani's office began to look more like an efficient operation than the result of a tornado.

Francesca looked at her watch for the fortieth time and said, "It's time." She picked up the phone and handed it to me.

I dialed. The desk sergeant picked up. I waited as he tried to page her. The desk sergeant had no idea where she was and I hung up.

"She's not there?" I said perplexed.

"I gathered." Francesca couldn't hide her disappointment.

"Let's go to the hospital. We can call from there. It'll give us something to do."

She nodded, grabbing the keys. In a few minutes we were on the subway headed for the hospital. I called from my cell. Still no Aunt J. We went to Max and Frieda's room. After exchanging greetings, Francesca announced, "Frau Helriegel will be home in the morning."

Max and Frieda brightened and then looking very satisfied, announced "So vill ve. The doctors tink ve are vell enough to be released."

"That's wonderful! But will you be able to go back to the house?"

Max and Frieda looked at each other, seeming to realize for the first time that the house was not livable for them.

"The police are still investigating the fire," I offered.

Francesca picked up on my lead. She ventured, "How bad was the damage that you could see?"

Max and Frieda shrugged, searching each other's faces. Frieda finally offered, "Max saw more dan I did. I vent to the telephone to call de fire brigade."

I smiled to myself at the quaint out-dated expressions they used for things. My fire engine was their fire brigade.

"Ja, ja, ven I opened de door to the basement, de smoke vas terrible. All de smoke detectors vere shrieking, but de sprinkler system in the hallway vas not vorking."

"Sprinkler system?" Francesca and I said this like well-rehearsed twins.

"Ja, the Frau had it installed two years ago. She said she was terrified of fire. Ever since de war, you know. She was in Berlin. Everything, everyone she loved vas destroyed." Max paused to compose himself. Frieda sniffled.

"Tell us what happened next," I said softly.

The elderly couple repeated their story from yesterday, adding that the power had gone out which also hampered Max's ability to see into the basement. His smoke inhalation seemed to be the result of trying to find the switch for the sprinkler system in the dark. The only new detail was the power failure resulting from the fire.

"Was there anything of value in the basement that Frau would want the police and firemen to look out for?" Francesca pressed.

Good, I thought, *perhaps Max and Frieda could tell us something*.

"Vine, a very extensive vine cellar, Frau always brought vine home vith her from Germany, France and Italy. She spent many hours in de basement in her vine cellar as she called it."

A dead end! I tried to keep the disappointment off my face as my brain struggled with this new puzzle. *What did wine have to do with any of this? Unless DiCristiani was her wine importer, as well as her gallery's manager. The connection between Frau Helriegel and DiCristiani was more mysterious than ever.*

The nurse came in. "You're going home tomorrow," she announced. Max and Frieda looked at her. "Ve have no home. Vhere vil ve go? The nurse looked at them and then at us.

"Frau Helriegel will be home by then. I'm sure she has thought about where you all will live until you can return to the brownstone," I said reassuringly.

"Max, vat is de date?" Frieda said urgently.

"February 17. Vy?" Before she could answer, he clapped his hands together in frustration. "Horst comes tomorrow also!"

"Who is Horst?" I asked, hoping fervently that it would be the right Horst.

"Horst is Frau's nephew. Dey are very close, in family, and in business. He always stays vith us." The two housekeepers began to talk excitedly about his visit, and how the fire would change all their plans.

Francesca and I exchanged furtive smiles. *Horst Blau, in New York. vell, vell, vell! I mean, well, well, well!* Max and Frieda chattered on about the homecoming. Max looked up at us. "You should be very interested in Herr, uh, Mister Blau."

I thought, *you should only know how much.*

Max continued, "He is giving a lecture at de Helmsley Palace Hotel. Very posh, I tink. The topic is—uh, making pictures right. Oh, Frieda, you tell dem. I can't think of de vords."

Frieda patted Max's hand. "Authentication is de vord. He vill speak about dose devices and methods dat are used to make sure dat a painting is not a fake, or a—a—. Ach, I can't remember de other vord."

"That would be wonderful," I said enthusiastically. "How can we get an invitation?"

"You vork for the Frau. She vill arrange it for you," Max assured us.

"It certainly would help me in my work at the gallery to be able to spot a forgery," Francesca added. Turning away from Max and Frieda she winked at me, giving me a quick thumbs-up.

Considering this ironic turn of events, I said, "We have to be going now. It will be nice to see you outside the hospital." We left.

"Let's try Aunt J again," I said as we passed through the lobby. This time, we were successful. "J here," she responded.

"Aunt J what's up with Francesca's tests?" I asked, not even trying to keep the tension out of my voice.

"They haven't come back yet, Annie. But I've been trying to find you. Lt Red called me from the house in Brooklyn. They've found something in the basement they want Francesca to see."

"What?" I demanded, my pulse pounding in the fingers that gripped the phone.

"He wouldn't tell me. Said it was too much to explain. He just wanted you to meet him in Brooklyn as soon as possible. Where are you?"

"At the hospital, visiting the housekeepers," I answered. "We . . ."

"Stay put," she cut me off. "Be out front. I'll pick you up."

Ten minutes later, we were on our way to Brooklyn with Aunt J in the Toyota.

"Red told me that they found a vault in the basement," she told us. "They had to contact the vault manufacturer to open it. Ordinarily, the manufacturer doesn't give out the combination, but since a crime was involved and the police had a search warrant, they had to."

"That's what Lt. Red wanted Francesca to see," I gasped.

"Annie, be patient!" she said, taking command.

"The vault was behind a wine rack that had fallen over during the fire. He said that we won't believe what's inside of it." Aunt J filled us in as we approached the Brooklyn Bridge, explaining how the vault was found by the firemen who were sifting through the ashes.

As Aunt J wove her way around the pot holes on the ramp to the bridge, I leaned back trying to ease the tension in my shoulders. The bridge has always been one of my most favorite of New York City's landmarks. I looked up as the intricate web of cables zipped by, making me dizzy. I could see the first pier emerging into view through the windshield and the huge American flag flapping majestically in the breeze.

Aunt J spoke, breaking the spell. "Francesca, did you know that people were afraid to cross this bridge in 1883 when it was completed?"

"Uh, yes. Didn't the guy who designed the bridge have to do some bizarre thing to prove it was okay?"

"He sure did. He convinced that famous circus guy, P.T. Barnum, to take the twenty-one elephants from his circus, which just happened to be in town, and walk them across the bridge just to show New Yorkers that it was safe."

"I guess it worked," muttered Francesca as we slowed to a crawl in the traffic.

I chuckled to myself, snuggling deeper into the seat as I recalled the first time my aunt told me that story. We rode the rest of the way in silence, giving up on the possibility that further conversation would help us find out what was in the vault.

I stared out of the window, watching the pedestrian lanes appear as we descended the ramp on the Brooklyn side of the bridge. Some brave souls trudged along, tensed against the wind. My gaze locked onto a cyclist weaving his way through the pedestrians, knifing his way into the wind at the speed afforded him by gravity.

"Good Lord! Isn't he cold?" Francesca said, apparently having locked onto the same subject.

"Oh, look. He's got a racing jersey from the New York Cycling Club. He must be in training," I concluded.

"One of the detectives in my office races with them. You know I've been on this bridge at all hours of the night, and I've seen racers training. It must be to avoid the traffic," Aunt J offered.

"What a way to stay in shape," I agreed.

We bounced off the bridge, crossed the plaza and made our way to Willow St.

Lt. Red's car was there as well as a cruiser. The brownstone looked forlorn. There were plywood sheets on the first floor windows, and the front door stood open, no warm light beckoning from within.

Aunt J flashed her badge at the police officer on guard at the door. We went in calling out to Lt. Red. A voice answered from the kitchen. "What took you?" He frowned at us. "C'mon down. I think you're going to be as dumbfounded as I was."

The basement timbers were charred, the smell of burnt wood so strong, it nearly made me sick. "You can see the path of the fire," Lt. Red explained. "We found the device that started the fire. As I said, a small explosive charge located near the furnace. In these cases, the fire marshal thinks that the origin of the fire is linked to a faulty oil burner. Very clever."

"This device was set off by a fuse activated by water dripping from the furnaces overflow valve. If Max and Frieda weren't in the house, it would have worked. Whoever did this must have known about the vault. I think it had to be the object of the crime."

We picked our way through the rubble and broken bottles left by the toppled wine rack. There, gaping open, was the door to the vault. The vault looked very much like a smaller version of a bank vault.

"Go on through," urged Lt. Red, who was behind us. We entered the vault. Lit up before us, was a mini-museum. We gasped.

There were easily twenty paintings, each illuminated from above by its own spotlight. The secret chamber, *I liked the sound of that*, was wood-paneled and softly lit. The floor was covered with rich carpets with oriental designs. I knew they were oriental because my mother had a passion for them and had tried to give me a little history lesson about them when I was a child. The paintings were mostly portraits. They were not the usual stiff poses you see in museums. The people in them seemed about to speak, or pick up a musical instrument or cut a flower from its bed. There were statues in marble and bronze placed around the chamber. A large pair of wing chairs bracketed a rosewood table with a brandy decanter and two snifters. I understood the meaning of the chamber to Frau Helriegel, but why two chairs, two brandy glasses? Did she have an accomplice amassing her collection?

As dumbstruck as I was, it was Francesca, who appeared the most spellbound.

"This is unbelievable," she uttered finally. "I recognize some of these paintings. These two were stolen two years ago from the Boston Museum." She walked from painting to painting. At one, she stopped, a moan escaping her lips as she reached out to touch the canvas. "This is my work," she cried in anguish. "That bastard, DiCristiani! He was passing my work off as authentic. This is some kind of secret collection."

"You're right, Miss Gabrielli," Lt. Red agreed.

"Call me Francesca," she murmured, shaking her head.

"The vault belongs to Frau Helriegel," he continued. "We found that out from the vault manufacturers."

The penny dropped for me. So that's why she hired DiCristiani. He was procuring these art pieces for her collection.

"I can't believe that nice old lady is a thief." Francesca shook her head again. "And Paolo, what does he know about this?"

"And did the Frau find out that this picture was a fake?" Aunt J speculated, pointing to Francesca's copy.

That would give her a motive for DiCristiani's murder. What an interesting idea had just popped into my head.

"I'm going to the airport to pick her up when she arrives tomorrow morning," announced Lt. Red. "She has a lot of questions to answer." Red looked at Aunt J, jerking his head toward the vault door and casting a glance at Francesca. They walked out together, talking in low tones, as Francesca and I continued to stare at the fabulous art pieces, identifying painters, admiring their agelessness.

When Francesca paused in front of her paintings, she gasped, tears welling in her eyes. "I did this painting," she told me, voice cracking. "I never could figure out why he wanted a copy of it," she continued, running her fingers lovingly across the canvas.

"It's pretty obvious to me, why he wanted it. It's so beautiful," I murmured staring at the picture.

It was a small canvas, only about fourteen by twenty-one. A girl sat on a window seat with a sketch pad on her lap, pencil poised above it. She looked out of the window at a single gnarled tree in a field of snow. I could have stepped easily through the frame to become that girl. The coincidence of this piece, a copy by Francesca, and my art lessons gave me an involuntary chill. Coincidences have always intrigued me. I looked at the girl in the painting. I thought about my ambition to learn how to draw and paint and I became aware of Francesca besides me, the artist herself.

"This painting is a mystery work," she breathed. "The experts think that it's an early Renoir, or perhaps one of his students. It's called simply, <u>Girl with Pencil Drawing</u>. It's the way the light is recreated here," she pointed out. "The harsh winter light reflects on the girl just perfectly to capture the moment she is just about to start sketching. When I was painting this, I could swear that her hand moved toward the paper just as I looked away from her to my own painting. This is probably my finest copy. Now look what it's all come to." Francesca looked at me, her shoulders slumping with frustration. "What does it all mean?" Francesca seemed to be at the end of her rope.

"I don't know," I muttered, my mind whirling with this strange new discovery, trying to tie all the facts together.

"Annie. Francesca. Let's go," called Aunt J. "Francesca, I'm afraid you'll have to go down to headquarters to give more blood."

Francesca's head snapped around to look at Aunt J. "Why?" she demanded.

"The hair was a match. Since DiCristiani was your employer, and Annie witnessed him man-handling you the morning of his murder, the hair, in itself, is not all that significant," she explained. "The preliminaries on the blood show a match in ABO and Rh blood groups. They have to go into blood enzymes, and possibly a DNA fingerprint, to rule you out entirely."

Francesca seemed to crumble at this news.

"Francesca, did you cut yourself. Were you bleeding from a cut when you went into the apartment?" J probed.

"No. I didn't have any cuts. I didn't even have my period," she confided.

Chapter 10
A MESSAGE ON E-MAIL

ON THE WAY HOME WE told Aunt J about our visit with Max and Frieda.

"The Brooklyn brownstone is about to receive a very interesting guest, Aunt J," I teased, trying to lighten the mood. "Want to know who?"

"Claude Monet, back from the dead?" she offered dryly.

Francesca grimaced at her attempt at humor. "Better than that," she countered.

"Okay. Who? I can't guess."

"Horst Blau!" I said triumphantly.

"Horst B—of Blau Electronics?" she demanded. "My, my, my!"

"Yup. He's the Frau's nephew, Aunt J. Doesn't it just get weirder all the time? He's giving a lecture on, you won't believe it, art authentication." After the laughter died down, I continued. "We're going, in the interests of the gallery, of course."

"Good work," Aunt J said, whistling through her teeth. "When Lt. Red picks up the Frau and Paolo at the airport tomorrow morning, he's going to give them a short version of what has happened so far. He'll bring them to their hotel, but after they are settled, he's planning to question her at the brownstone. He wants you there, Francesca, as well. I'll take you to headquarters in the morning for the blood work up, and then we'll go to meet them."

"What about me?" I demanded.

"I'm going to tie you to a kitchen chair, so you'll stay home," Aunt J teased.

"Could we stop you from coming? If I said you couldn't come, you'd disguise yourself as a fireman and come anyway."

"You're right about everything except the disguise. I hope that I would choose a more interesting disguise than a fireman," I said in mock indignation.

"Miss Tillery? What did that ABO, Rh stuff mean about the blood tests?" Francesca asked, sobering up the conversation.

"All human blood falls into four major categories, A, B, AB and O. There are several other less known categories, like Rh. What causes the different blood groupings is the presence of protein markers. Protein markers are chemicals that can be identified in the blood. DiCristiani's blood is Type O, the most common type. The mystery blood is another type. That's why they think it might belong to the killer. It was found at the crime scene, and its type is different from the victim's. Your blood tests the same as the mystery blood for the major groups. But that blood type represents a large group of people.

So now, they're testing for the more specific blood markers. If they find even one dissimilarity, there is no match."

"Thanks," Francesca replied, crumpling back down in the seat.

When we got home, Aunt J went to take a hot shower. "Francesca, I've got to check my e-mail," I said. She seemed not to be in any mood to relax, and I didn't know what to do to calm her fears.

"Yeah, I noticed your computer. That's cool. I use the one at the library in the Metropolitan," Francesca replied. "I'll just go watch TV then."

"I'm not expecting a love letter," I explained, embarrassed. "Come with me."

We went to my room, and logged on to my e-mail. Ty and I used e-mail rather than Facebook or other social networks because he emailed from the lab at school and the scientists at the lab felt more secure if students were not putting out personal information on their computer system.

"Good. There's mail, one from Ty and one from the N.Y. Public Library System. That's for a paper I'm doing in school. Let's see what Ty has to say. Whoops, and one from my parents who are in Turkey."

"Wow, Turkey! I always wanted to go there. Plenty of art to study. What are your parents doing there?"

"My dad works for the State Department and he is on assignment in Istanbul. My mom is struggling with depression and alcoholism. She just got out of rehab a few months ago. Dad thought it best to have her there. She has a doctorate in archeology and Dad pulled some strings to get her a job at a university in Istanbul."

Francesca gave me an appraising glance. "Don't you miss them?" She added, "How tough for your mom."

My old defenses took over. "My life is here. My dad has always worked for State, so I got used to not seeing him. As for my mother . . ." I trailed off trying to put into words what I felt about her. "I have a hard time dealing with my mother, and it causes friction between me and Dad. For now, long distance is working for me."

"I didn't mean to pry," Francesca murmured and changing the mood urged, "Why don't you see what Ty has to say." She got up and browsed through my book shelves, relieving us both of the problem of saying anything more.

I clicked on his message. The computer screen flashed the gibberish associated with all e-mail messages. I stared at it, as I waited for the message to come on-screen. Something about the gibberish caught my attention, something familiar.

The message flashed onto the screen, breaking my train of thought. It simply said *If you're home 2/17, 6-7 PM, IM me. Love Ty.* I looked at my watch. It was 6:20. I hit Reply. The screen for my message painted across the screen. I typed "COME ON IN TY, and waited.

My e-mail chime sounded and his message appeared. *"Switch to chat."* I did with a few clicks and drags of the mouse.

I miss you, he typed.

Me too, I replied.

The back of my mind kept nagging me. What was it that I had seen on the e-mail message page that struck a memory chord? *Ty, my computer wizard, I have a favor to ask of you.* I banged out on impulse. *All that gibberish that appears before each message on the introduction page to the messages, what does it mean? Can you go through it with me, item by item?*

I waited. The reply appeared in the chat box. *Sure. Print one from my last message. You can look at it as I describe it.*

I did what he asked, and placed the sheet in front of me, looking at it line by line. It hit me! The numbers and letters! They were familiar. I went to my jacket where I'd stuffed the list that I had memorized from Frau Helriegel's desk. Two of the number/letter combinations had the same pattern as the number sequence on my print-out. I quickly typed a message to Ty. *Just tell me what the sequence of numbers and letters mean.*

His reply came back. *That's the e-mail address in ASCII codes. It's computer language.*

"The Eureka piece! Those numbers Lt. Red sent to his computer team were e-mail addresses. They'll have the same answer soon." I turned to see what Francesca's reaction was. The computer had sent her fast asleep.

I went back to the chat box. *Can anyone translate those number/letter sequences into e-mail addresses?*

He replied, *You need to know the ASCII code. You can find it in any basic computer language text.*

Do you have one? If I send you a couple of sequences, can you translate them for me?

I can, he replied.

Oh. I love this guy, I thought. *Not only sexy, but truly a genius.*

What's up? I'll only do it if you let me know why.

I explained, telling him, *I'll type the list for you. You work on the codes and you'll have a capsulized version of my last few days in the box when you're done.*

Roger. He replied.

I went to find Aunt J and the complete list. When I explained what Ty had said, she picked up the phone to call the lieutenant. "Keep Ty on line, and I'll call Red. He has the complete list."

Back in my room Francesca slept on, succumbing to the tension of the past few days. Ty had already finished the two sequences I had given him. I told him that I was waiting for the rest. We chatted. His research project was almost done. It was snowing in Boston. I said I couldn't remember such a snowy winter in N.Y. He typed out *I love you,* and Aunt J appeared with the list. I quickly typed it and sent it.

I tapped my pencil on the desk, impatient for Ty to finish working on J's list. Seeing that Francesca was still sleeping, I stopped tapping the desk and moved on to whiling away the time by surveying the memorabilia hung on the walls of my room. I skimmed along the items on my cork board, pictures of Ty and me at Christmas in front of the tree in Rockefeller Center, of us sailing off the coast of Fire Island, and a copy of Dan's Papers. Ty's Uncle Doc had given it to me on my first day on Fire Island. I had looked at the article about Fire Island in Dan's Papers so often that the map of the island felt like a limp Kleenex. Thinking about meeting Ty on Fire Island last summer, solving the strange mystery of the local ghost, and falling in love made me melt like chocolate chips in the microwave.

I typed the long e-mail I had promised. Twenty minutes later, during the eleven o'clock news, the computer screen flickered. After the usual clicks and drags, the list appeared with a message from Ty.

These appear to be real. I sent a dummy message to one of them, and the computer didn't tell me it was bogus. It sent the message.

Thanks, Ty. As soon as I know more, I'll let you know.

Roger.

Read your e-mail. I signed off.

"Annie, how did you figure that out?" Aunt J wanted to know. I tried to explain that I was dumb not to realize what those numbers meant all along. I e-mail so often that I see them almost every day. It was just tonight, seeing them for the first time since the list appeared, that it clicked.

Francesca struggled to wake up, our conversation having disturbed her nap. "What happened?"

"Go to bed, Francesca. We'll explain tomorrow," Aunt J urged gently.

"Okay," she mumbled. "I didn't realize how tired I was."

Deserted by my two partners in crime-busting, I sat for a while going over the last two days. My mind churned. *How did Horst Blau fit?* I was sure he was an important piece. Finally, wishing Ty were here, I turned out the light, said a prayer for Francesca's blood tests to turn out okay and I went to sleep.

Chapter 11
THE SPOILS OF WAR

THE NEXT MORNING WAS A snowy traffic nightmare. We struggled from home to police headquarters downtown, and then across the Brooklyn Bridge again. I traveled across that bridge more times in the last few days then in all the rest of my life.

To my surprise in the midst of all the snow, a stream of cyclists in their club uniforms was making its way across the bridge in the bike lane which had been plowed.

There they are again! Boy, that's dedication. I leaned back into the warm seat shivering at the thought of being out on the bridge in all this snow.

When we got to the brownstone the front door had been replaced and the electricity had been fully restored. We knocked on the door. Frau Helriegel opened it herself, letting us into the chilly interior. "Our only heat is from the fireplaces. A new furnace is coming tomorrow."

"Lt. Red will be here shortly," Aunt J explained.

"I have made coffee, would you like some? Max and Frieda are trying to make the kitchen workable. Come this way."

"Coffee would be lovely, thank you," said Aunt J. in a gentle manner that caught me off-guard. The Frau could possibly be a murderer. I was confused.

Max and Frieda were glad to see us, and happy to be home. "Dis is better dan a hotel. Ve vill have de place in good order very soon."

Frau Helriegel smiled weakly. She was pale. We drank our coffee to make up for the uncomfortable silence. Francesca looked around, jumping at every sound. I didn't need to ask her why she was so jumpy. Where was Paolo?

Mercifully, Lt. Red showed up within ten minutes. We exchanged greetings. Lt. Red turned to Frau Helriegel saying, "Shall we proceed to your museum?" He gestured toward the basement stairs. She led the way, posture erect, her face a stiff mask. There was deep pain in her eyes.

We traveled the same path as the previous night, through the rubble in the basement, and into the vault room. Paolo was there photographing, and taking notes on the paintings.

"I have asked him to do this for me. I would like to look at the photographs of these treasures from time to time in the days that I have left."

Paolo looked up at this, anguish for his grandmother's disgrace apparent on his face. He quickly composed himself, giving us a brief smile.

"Paolo knew nothing of this collection. It was probably the best kept secret in the Western World," she explained.

"How did you acquire this collection?" Aunt J asked quietly.

Frau Helriegel sat down in a wing-backed chair that obviously had allowed her to sit amid her treasures, when she visited the vault. This had been the wine cellar that Max and Frieda thought was occupying the attention of their mistress.

With a deep sigh Frau Helriegel's story unfolded. "I was a nurse in Germany during the war. I am actually Czechoslovakian, but when the Nazis invaded my homeland, they took all the skilled people back to the Fatherland, where we could help them do their dirty work.

I survived the war, the Nazis, and the terrible bombing at the end. It was a miracle to me. I was lucky to have my nursing skills, as well. The Allies drafted all the able-bodied, like me, to help with the enormous task of caring for the sick, injured, and starving. As Dickens once said, 'These were the worst of times' and, as it turned out, also the 'best of times.'

During the eighteen-to twenty-hour days that I worked in the hospital, I met an American officer. He was in charge of the dispatch of displaced persons in our sector. He spoke German, an invaluable talent at that time. His name was Robert Renz. We fell in love. I was never so happy."

The elderly lady paused. I thought she was going to faint, but she summoned some inner strength and continued. "He stayed through the next two years and became friends with Heinrich Blau, who had been a minor advisor to the Ministry of Art for the Nazi government. Heinrich had cooperated fully with the Allies from the start. That kept him out of jail."

"They had two major areas of common interest, electronics and art. My Robert came from a wealthy American family.

He liked Heinrich's ideas about the future of electronic communications. To make a long story short, he loaned Heinrich the money to start Blau Electronics."

There was no sound in the room. Everyone was spellbound by the Frau's tale. She rubbed her brow and continued. "At the end of his tour, Robert went back to his wife and family in America. I always knew that was to be. I didn't care. I wanted him for as long as I could have him. I wouldn't trade those days for anything. Not even to relieve the pain I felt for losing him." Paolo had come to stand behind his grandmother, his hands resting lightly on her shoulders.

I looked around to see if anyone could see my tears. There were many glistening eyes in the room. I thought of Ty again and wished he were here with me.

Frau Helriegel went on, "In those last days, he left my side only once, returning with a large package. In it were four paintings. Three of them, you see in this room. He told me that they were gifts from the Nazis, for the trouble they had caused me. Later, he confided that he had gotten them from Heinrich and that I must keep them a secret. He wanted me to have them in case I needed money. I could sell them in the right places, for a lot of cash. Because the Nazis had confiscated these pieces, they were worth many times their true value. If I ever needed to, Heinrich would arrange a sale. This was his legacy to me. I sold one painting. Investments after the war made me a rich woman."

"Where did the other paintings come from?" asked Lt. Red.

"It was easy to acquire them, once you knew the network. There were several of us. And soon we became a 'club,' known only to each other. Even my husband, whom I married two years after Robert left, never knew."

"Frau Helriegel," Lt. Red pushed on, when we questioned you before you left for Germany, I showed you a list of numbers. You told me they meant nothing to you. Do you want to change your mind about that now?"

"How did you get into my vault?" she asked.

"Once we determined that the fire was arson, the vault manufacturer had no choice but to give us the combination. I had the list and recognized the combination immediately," Lt. Red's replied.

Aunt J continued, "We traced the phone numbers, and know who they belong to, but didn't understand what they had in common. We're hoping you will help us with that. It will not go well for you if you don't cooperate. Buying stolen art is a crime."

"We only figured out what the other numbers were last night," said Lt. Red.

I cleared my throat. Red looked at me. "They're e-mail addresses," I stated simply.

"I won't even go there!" He smiled. "This computer stuff is best left to the 'user' generation. My team came up with answer as soon as they saw the list."

"We don't know whose addresses they are yet," said Aunt J. "Can't you help us, Frau?"

"I must see my list of owners to tell you that," she answered, her voice dull with resignation.

"But, you had that list in your desk," Aunt J protested. "You must know what they are."

"I copied that list from one I had seen in John DiCristiani's office at the gallery. He was clever, but sloppy. I went there one night to snoop, once I realized how evil he was," she said bitterly, "It was taped to the bottom of a drawer. I cannot understand where he got hold of this information." She shook her head, "In fact, how did you know I had the list?"

"I saw it on the desk in your parlor when I was admiring a painting," I replied, noting to myself that it was no lie.

At last Francesca spoke up. "Did you know that my painting was a forgery when you bought it?"

"Not then. But I had it authenticated by someone the club trusts. He found it to be a forgery."

Horst Blau jumped into my head. *Was he the authenticator of the painting?*

"What did you do about it?" Red asked.

"I confronted DiCristiani. He told me about Francesca's work, that she thought her work was being used legitimately. I threatened to expose him. He threatened to expose all of us."

"How did he know about all of you?" Aunt J asked.

I couldn't help but admire how Aunt J's and Lt. Red's questions were getting the information they needed.

"I said he was clever. If I expressed interest in stolen art, what about my business associates? He knew who they were because they also purchased legitimate pieces. Most of what he sold was legitimate, but the big money was in the stolen pieces. It was just a matter of making the right contacts and offers. I suppose that is why he had that list taped to his desk drawer."

"Did he know about the vault?" Red continued.

"He must have, at least, suspected that it was here," she answered.

"We think that was the reason for the arson. Did you know he owned the building next door?" Aunt J looked at Frau Helriegel.

"Ach, so! The construction project," she smiled wryly.

"Did you kill John DiCristiani?" Aunt J said this very softly.

The Frau looked at her hands, lying limp in her lap. "Whoever killed him, my hat goes off to them. He deserved what he got."

"Did *you* kill him?"

"No," she said, simply.

"Do you know who did?"

"There are many with the right reasons, don't you agree?" she responded. She reached up and grasped Paolo's hand.

"What will happen to my grandmother," Paolo asked anxiously. "She is . . ." Frau Helriegel shushed him.

"She will have to give back the pieces. She will have to cooperate with the authorities. After that it's the judge's decision. Considering her age, and lack of other criminal activities, I don't believe there will be jail time," Aunt J told Paolo soberly.

"There can be no trips out of this city, Frau, until this is settled. I must have your promise. We can perhaps waive bail after you're charged."

"You have it. I don't feel much like traveling now." She looked up at her grandson, who attempted a smile. "It is quite cold here. Can we go upstairs now?"

We filed back upstairs. Frau Helriegel retired to her room with Max and Frieda in close attendance. Paolo turned to Francesca, "Have your tests cleared you of that bastard's murder?"

"Not yet," Francesca managed, her eyes downcast. "I've got to get back to work," she added. We left the brownstone and its air of gloom. It was good to be out in the air. Lt Red and Aunt J left us off at the gallery on their way to headquarters.

The gallery was quiet and we set to work. "The list of suspects is growing," I offered this as a crumb of encouragement, knowing how down Francesca was. Even I was tiring of my little-miss-sunshine act. I just wished those tests would come back negative. She was shuffling through the mail.

"First, we have Frau Helriegel, who couldn't afford to be exposed, as well as all her friends. Then, there's Horst, the young protector of their empire."

"I am assuming that he is the art authenticator for the 'club'," Francesca added. "She didn't mention his name, but it certainly fits."

"Yes, I saw it that way too. He needed to eliminate the interloper. Do you think Horst has a collection of his own?" I asked.

"He must," Francesca declared emphatically. "He must have inherited his father's collection. Frau Helriegel said his father was the source of the original collection."

"Is his father dead?" I asked.

'We can find out. But, why else do you think he would have become an expert at art forgery?"

"Yes. It seems pretty obvious when you put it that way," I agreed.

"Don't forget Mark DiCristiani," Francesca added, warming up to my idea of listing suspects. "He stood to benefit in a huge financial way by offing his father. Let me tell you, they had some wicked arguments. I don't like him. He's a real creep, just like his father. Rest his soul," she added with a short little laugh. Francesca could be very harsh, and I didn't like that side of her.

"Look, Annie! We received an invitation to Horst Blau's lecture at the Helmsley Palace."

"We're definitely going," I said. "We can ask some questions and get an idea of what he's like. Maybe we can find out if he has a collection of his own."

"Sure. I'll just say, Hey, Horsey, can you give us any tips on locating secret vaults belonging to our art customers?" Francesca shook her head.

I pushed on, "Maybe he'll slip and mention some artwork that he's authenticated, and that we know is stolen."

"Forget it, Annie. These people have a lot of practice keeping the secret."

I gave up my line of reasoning, but having been presented with the opportunity to see and possibly talk to Horst Blau, I couldn't let go of trying to find a way to get him to divulge something that would help us to solve the mystery of DiCristiani's death.

Francesca, having discounted my comments, was carefully examining the invitation. "It's formal, though," she added wrinkling her nose.

"Great! Aunt J has a closet full of formals. She gets invited to lots of fancy parties. Police politics. We can borrow two of her outfits. It'll be cool."

"Not your typical cop, huh. I didn't realize there's such glamour." She laughed, lightening up a bit," Sorry, I'm so grouchy. I'm worried. Yes. I want to go, if just to get my mind off this murder. It will certainly be strange to get all dressed up. Just don't take any pictures. My friends will think I've lost my mind." We laughed, glad to be out of the gloom for a minute.

"For a murder suspect, you sure sound giddy."

We both turned to see Mark DiCristiani standing at the door, grinning an evil little smirk.

"We're working on including you in our happy little circle, Mr. Mark," Francesca mouthed off at him. "You had a lot more reason to off Daddy than I did. If things go well, we'll tie you into the arson at Frau Helriegel's."

His smirk drooped. "Oh, I'm still working on having you barred from this gallery," he countered.

"How, Mark?" Your father didn't own the place."

"These are his things that you feel free to be going through," he said.

"These things are Frau Helriegel's business records," I pointed out.

"My lawyer will have them confiscated as my father's personal effects," he argued. He was shifting from one foot to the other, eyes darting around the room.

Francesca grabbed one of the desk drawers and dumped the contents into a carton on the floor. She kicked it at him violently. "Here, take them now, you jerk. We're finished with them. We know all we want to know."

He backed toward the door. I'll be back with a court order," he sneered. "You two babes better be careful. This is a dangerous city. All kinds of accidents can happen, in the subway or on a dark street. Nasty things can happen to young girls. Some are never seen again."

"I'd be real careful about the threats I make, Mark," I said this with more confidence than I felt. Inside, I was shaking and I don't know how the words got out.

"Just be careful, Babe." He turned and left.

Chapter 12
Introducing Horst

It was getting dark and Mark's surprise visit made every shadow in the room ominous, every noise in the quiet gallery a potential threat. I made us cups of hot chocolate and we tried to dispel Mark DiCristiani's threat. We weren't having much success. I remembered the two men who had chased us in the subway the first day of the art class.

"What would those two guys who chased us from the art school have done to us, if they'd caught us?" I asked Francesca.

"Probably cornered us in some alley and threatened us. Left a few marks to remind us," she replied grimly.

"Remind us of what?" I asked, realizing that I didn't know what kind of threat we had posed at the time.

"Annie, I knew about the copies. I think they suspected that I knew about Mr. D's other illegal operations."

"Did you?"

"No. I didn't care about anything he did outside the gallery. I just knew he was mob connected."

"But now Mark knows that you and I know a lot. Mark is DiCristiani's son and heir to all his operations. We must be quite a threat to him." It was beginning to sink in, exactly how ugly this all was.

I remembered Mark's uneasiness as he threatened us and wondered why he was so nervous. He seemed to be looking for something. Francesca began to rummage around in the desk for something. I watched her absently when suddenly she smacked a small black address book on the desk. As I stared at her, wondering what she had found, she tucked the little book into a planter among the lush leaves of an arrowhead plant.

"No one will look here, and I don't want to take a chance of losing it, or worse," she declared. My stomach lurched at her words and the idea of being cornered by Mark in some dark alley. *Was it the book he had been after all along?*

"Just in case he comes back," she added. "We haven't had a chance to look at it yet. I forgot about it until now."

Good thinking!" I agreed as we grabbed our coats to go home. The thought of getting dressed up and going to a glamorous affair had real appeal after the events of the last few days.

We walked towards the subway, as usual, picking our way carefully through the icy streets. It was almost dark and people were going home from work. I was glad for the throngs of pedestrians tonight. Mark DiCristiani's threat had unnerved me. I kept looking over my shoulder.

"What's the matter, Annie?" Francesca said nervously looking around.

"Just jumpy, I guess."

"Are we being followed?"

"I don't think so. The streets are full of people. We're pretty safe, I hope."

A car pulled up along side us, nearly giving me a heart attack.

"Jump in girls. I thought you might need a ride home." It was Aunt J.

"Oh, J, I love you!" I gave her a big kiss once inside the car.

"You look nervous, Annie. Anything else happen?" she inquired, threading her way into the uptown traffic.

We told her about the visit from Mark. She frowned, "Until this case is settled, I want you to check in every hour. No more subways. I'll have you picked up and dropped off when necessary."

"But . . ."

"No buts. A man has been murdered. A house has been torched. You've been threatened. I'm going to give you a special cell phone. You just have to push the 7 key and hold it down. It's automatically keyed into a special police emergency number. I will alert them to find me and Lt. Red, no matter what."

I knew when not to fight Aunt J's protective instincts. Actually, I felt relieved.

"We got an invitation to Horst Blau's lecture on art forgeries tonight. Will you help us out with some clothes? It's formal and we're late."

"Certainly, and I'll be your chauffeur, as well."

I'm more than a half foot taller than Aunt J. Her dresses only fit me if I planned on wearing a mini. Francesca, on the other hand, was a perfect size match. She could have her pick of her formal attire. As we entered the apartment, I mentally browsed through my own wardrobe. Realizing that I had nothing appropriate, I followed my aunt and Francesca into the master bedroom.

"This little black dress is beautiful. May I wear this one?"

"Perfect," said Aunt J. "With these silver shoes and bag."

"Wear your hair up, Francesca. Then you can wear these dangly black beaded earrings."

Aunt J burrowed into the closet, coming out with a shocking pink satin mini dress with matching long jacket. "Don't you have a pair of white satin pants, Annie?"

"Yeah, they would look great with this set," I agreed.

We dressed. When Aunt J wore the pink satin set, the jacket was finger-tip length. On me, it was stylishly at the hip-line of my trousers.

The three of us managed to pile Francesca's and my hair on top of our heads, with carefully placed stray tendrils falling about our necks.

"Those outfits require some makeup. Don't you think?" Aunt J suggested.

Fifteen minutes later, we both looked ten years older, and felt very sophisticated.

"Make sure you take the invitation, Francesca," I reminded her.

"Take some money," Aunt J reminded me. "All set?"

We set off for the car. The night was frigid but clear, and blessedly windless. I thought I would freeze to death without my boots, mittens and hat.

"Turn the heater on, J," I urged.

"Ah, the price of looking beautiful," she laughed. "And you do look beautiful. Both of you," she remarked proudly. "Is Paolo going to this lecture?" she asked.

"You know, I never thought to ask," Francesca exclaimed. "His grandmother looked so devastated, that I just couldn't imagine him leaving her side."

"No. It wasn't the time to intrude with such a seemingly mundane question," agreed Aunt J.

"But Paolo is Horst's nephew," I pointed out. "I would guess this is like a family affair. I bet Paolo will be there. He was just too preoccupied to think of mentioning it to us."

There was a snarl of traffic in front of the Helmsley Palace Hotel when we arrived. There were so many flash cameras going off, it looked like a light show at a dance club.

"Horst Blau is an international celebrity," Aunt J offered. "He is considered one of the most eligible bachelors in Europe. The paparazzi follow him everywhere."

"How come we've never heard about him then?" I wanted to know.

"Probably because he's not a movie star, just filthy rich," Aunt J explained.

Finally, it was our turn to get out. To my surprise, the paparazzi took our picture. "Call me for a ride home." The Toyota slipped away, leaving Aunt J's stern admonition hanging in the air.

"Okay!" We waved excitedly as she pulled away, leaving us to the glamour of the evening.

We hurried into the warmth of the hotel lobby. Lobby was an understatement! When they say Helmsley Palace, the emphasis should definitely be placed on the palace part.

The cavernous lobby had a central crystal chandelier that was the size of a two-car garage. It sparkled and twinkled with what must be thousands of prisms, and it was flanked by four smaller ones, just as glittery. The tiles on the floor shone softly with every color that marble was found in. Rich oriental carpets were placed in alcoves around the central hall along with potted palms. Overstuffed chairs upholstered in tapestries and velvets made sumptuous conversation islands.

"Wow, this is too gorgeous!" Francesca breathed, busy scanning the arriving guests.

"Lovely, but give me a ski lodge in Vermont any day," I observed.

"Hmmm, with Ty?" Francesca winked at me.

"Ummm, Yessss!" I replied, enjoying the moment.

"I thought we were going to be overdressed at first," Francesca said, looking about her in awe. "Now I'm sorry I didn't wear a long ball gown."

"We look fine," I said firmly. "New York chic."

Signs for the lecture were placed in strategic locations. Coats checked, hair and makeup adjusted, we set off for the cocktail reception. Two club sodas in hand, we tried to look comfortable and not too obvious about celebrity spotting.

"There's Paolo!" Francesca waved excitedly, dragging me off in his direction.

"Paolo! Mr. Helriegel!" she called as he headed away from us. At last he heard us and turned on his heels.

"Annie! Francesca! What a pleasant surprise. But I should have known you would want to come. Now I feel like a dope. I should have offered to take you when I saw you at the house this morning," he declared, embarrassed.

"You had a lot on your mind," Francesca said sympathetically.

"Yes, I did. I still do. I find myself doubting what has happened, and my grandmother is brokenhearted. She is not physically well either."

"She didn't look well," I admitted, and ventured, "You must know our honored speaker well."

"Yes. He and my father are very close. He introduced my mother and father, was best man at the wedding, and all that. Being with Uncle Horst is like holding onto a live electric wire. Everything is an adventure. He taught me to scuba dive in Turkey when I was a boy. We've had many good times."

"Sounds like a great guy," Francesca said smiling warmly at Paolo.

"I'll introduce you after the lecture. Meanwhile, let me escort you to the hors d'oeuvres," he offered, taking each of us by an arm. "You both look smashing. Everyone is looking at us!"

I was looking at the man of the hour. I recognized him from the photographs in the hotel lobby. He was tall, at least six foot two, very blond with eyes as blue as aquamarine crystal. The eyes were riveting, like blue ice. He was startlingly handsome in his tuxedo and black tie, talking in an animated fashion with an equally gorgeous middle-aged woman dressed in dark green velvet.

Taking in more of the scene, I noticed how many couples and groups of people were having their pictures taken. There were other less glamorous individuals in the room. One burly gentleman in a tux that was a little too small for him was talking into his sleeve. I could just see a thin transparent plastic wire leading from his collar to an earpiece that looked like a hearing aid. There were other men and, I think, one woman who appeared to be acting and dressed in a similar manner. Their eyes canvassed the room continually. These must be security guards, Horst's protection services. Not surprising given the amount of money tied up here.

"Caviar?" Paolo offered.

"Ugh, no thanks. Too fishy for me!" I protested. Francesca, on the other hand, accepted. As Paolo handed her the cracker with caviar, I caught the gleam of a large ring on his hand.

"Oh, Paolo. I've never seen you wear that ring before," Francesca exclaimed as she reached for his hand to admire it. It was a large gold signet ring.

"Uncle Horst gave it to me at my college graduation. I don't wear it most of the time because of my studies. All that lab work."

"What are you going to do now, Paolo?" Francesca asked.

"I'm going back to medical school when the inter-term is over."

"Who's going to take care of the gallery?" she asked.

"My grandmother intended to offer the job to you, if you worked out after the first couple of months. I don't see why that should change."

"You said that your grandmother's health is not good. Who will take care of her?" I asked.

"Max and Frieda."

"But, they're very old too," I protested.

"My mother is coming to stay for a couple of months. If you decide to take the gallery job, she will be your boss."

"I thought you were really interested in the gallery." Francesca sounded disappointed.

"I am, but I want to be a physician, probably specializing in infectious diseases. I love my grandmother, but the gallery was never meant as a career for me."

"Where is medical school?" Francesca asked, eying Paolo unselfconsciously.

"Right here in New York. Cornell," he said, smiling back at her just as unabashedly.

"Oh. Then I can call you up to help me when I have a problem with the gallery," she said coyly.

"No, you can call my mother if you have a problem with the gallery. You can call me to talk about anything else." His eyes twinkled as he leaned down to kiss her lightly on the lips.

Ty would do that, I thought wistfully. Francesca looked radiant, standing on tip-toe, she kissed him back.

The lights dimmed twice, indicating that we were to take our seats for the lecture. We found them, sharing Paolo between us.

Horst launched into his lecture using a very clever interactive Smart Board presentation developed especially for the lecture. From what little I know about computer graphics, I could see that his was an intricate piece of work. The large screen at the front of the auditorium showed us what was on the computer screen. As Horst pointed to various parts of the painting he used as an illustration, the screen changed to show different techniques used in the authentication of an art piece. These could be manipulated on the screen to show step-by-step how each procedure worked.

As his hand moved up and down, I caught the flash of a ring on his right hand. "There are two aspects that are investigated when an art piece's authenticity is in question." His English was impeccable and barely accented. The ring continued to flash with his emphatic gestures. I was becoming hypnotized by his wonderful voice and the twinkling glint of the ring flashing at the bottom of the colorful screen. It was a great opportunity for me to hear this lecture because I wanted to know how to differentiate between real and fake art. It might shed some light on what was happening to Francesca.

He began, "First, an expert on a particular artist is called in to examine the style of that artist. This investigation sometimes leads to a decision based on a matter of opinion as the expert studies that artist's style. It is often, however, the more scientific aspects that can discriminate between the copy and the original. Here we can analyze paint pigments, signatures, finishes, canvases, and the presence of other paintings behind the one we see on the canvas. Spectrographic analysis, carbon dating, and x-ray radiography are the tools we use here, even the electron microscope."

He was an interesting and accomplished speaker. He was also quite sexy. As he became more technical, I noticed Francesca taking notes with a pad provided at the table. My mind kept wandering to the man. I was searching to see if I could find some small piece of evidence in a gesture or a look that would help me to decide if Horst could kill. He had every reason to get rid of DiCristiani, but he had every reason not to risk his incredibly blessed life style by killing a scum like DiCristiani.

He could have hired a hit man. Would he be ruthless enough to kill another human being? A man who had a son? It was difficult to reconcile that idea with the cultured individual on the stage. Speaking of the son, it was easy to put Mark DiCristiani in the role of murderer, even of his own father. The explosion at Frau Helriegel's house occurred after DiCristiani's murder. The arson was obviously connected to DiCristiani. He owned the house next door. Did he buy it to snoop or to steal the contents of the vault? Did Mark know about the work on the Willow St. house? If not who ordered the work to continue after DiCristiani's murder? How did the arsonists get into Frau Helriegel's basement?

Applause broke into my thoughts. The lecture was over. When the audience quieted down, Horst announced that he would take questions. A platinum blond woman in a low cut silver gown asked in a husky voice, "Do you give private lessons?" The audience laughed!

Horst replied, "Not on the subject of art." The audience roared. I wondered if the woman was a plant to soften up the audience and keep up interest.

Francesca, who had been glued to Horst's every word, raised her hand. It took ten minutes before she was recognized. An usher came over to her with the microphone.

"How do forgers make paintings look old, Mr. Blau?" she asked.

What an odd question, I thought. *She's done it herself. Is she testing him?*

"There are various techniques. It is usually done with several coats of a spray-on fixative and dirt. Exposure to heat will produce the crazing one often sees in old paintings."

"But the spray-on fixatives won't stand up to the spectrographic analysis," Francesca countered. "It will show them to be modern materials."

"That's how we trip up the forger," Horst replied. "It is almost impossible to get the right combination of paint pigments and other materials, along with technique. Aging the painting may look authentic to the eye, but it usually gives the painting away as a forgery."

"Is it possible to reproduce the materials used by artists, say, of the Renaissance?" Francesca pressed.

"Only if you were in a position to have the chemical analyst's report of originals at your disposal. Then you have to have the chemistry skills to reproduce those materials. You would still have to pass the scrutiny of the expert who is looking at the artist's style."

"How then, do so many forgeries show up?"

"So many don't. There are, in comparison to the number of paintings in museums, very few forgeries. Most of those got by in the past because museums didn't have access to the techniques I have just explained. Private collectors would have to incur the cost of all these technologies, which, I failed to mention, is considerable. Put this cost on top of the original price of a masterpiece, it is a quite sizable sum."

"Thank you." Francesca sat down.

"Nice try!" I whispered behind Paolo's back, realizing that she was trying to get him to slip up. By drawing him out, he might mention something that would click for us. What could he say, except an admission that he had a private collection that he had authenticated. I felt frustrated.

The questions went on for another ten minutes. Horst announced that his secretary would be taking donations for his private charity, scholarships for needy artists.

"I should apply," Francesca laughed, "I could use my copy from Frau Helriegel's vault in my portfolio."

Paolo said, "Let's go meet my uncle." We wove our way through the throng of art patrons and admirers, drinking in the delicious aromas of expensive perfumes and after-shave. Gorgeous dresses swished out of our way as we said "excuse me" to each person in our way. I felt as if we were in the middle of my paint palette, there were so many vibrantly colored clothes.

"Paolo! My young friend!" Horst exclaimed as we approached. He shook Paolo's hand and then hugged him, kissing both cheeks in the European way. "What have you got for my arthritis?" he teased.

"I want you to meet two friends of mine, Uncle Horst." Paolo introduced us. For an instant, the eyes bored into us, the icy stare like a laser. Just as quickly, the face warmed into an affable grin. "Paolo, you must give me some pointers on how you acquired these two fantastic beauties. I am impressed."

Feeling like a melon about to be squeezed, I smiled politely, sensing Francesca stiffen beside me. The ring that had caught my attention before winked at me, teasing me. I wanted to see it, to judge if my fascination was warranted. But the hand slipped deftly into his pants pocket before I could take a peek at it.

I extended my hand for him to shake, hoping the hand would reappear. Instead he took mine in his other hand and kissed it, and then turned to do the same to Francesca. I smiled to myself. *Nice try, Annie.*

Horst lingered over Francesca. "There is great danger in forging art pieces, Miss. Gabrielli. Many collectors pay great sums for their acquisitions. These rich people are also powerful. They do not like to be tricked."

He smiled as he said this, but his message enveloped us with a chill. Obviously, Horst knew more about us then we had bargained for. Not so surprising when you thought of his connection to Frau Helriegel.

Paolo came to the rescue, "Come, I'll drive you home."

We gratefully accepted a graceful way to bow out, and escape the chill of Horst's words.

Chapter 13
TROUBLE IN BROOKLYN

AS WE WAITED FOR PAOLO in the car, Francesca whispered, "Annie, did anything strike you about Horst Blau? Something oddly familiar?"

"No. He is charismatic, charming, sexy, incredibly well-dressed, reeks money, but . . . What do you mean? Like a déjà vu thing?

"Yes," she said staring into my face. "I . . . There is something familiar about him to me."

"You've probably seen his picture in the paper," I offered.

"Maybe, but I have the feeling that it's important, and I can't put my finger on what it is." She snuggled into the warm car seat, chewing her lip and frowning in the effort to remember something.

Paolo got in and as he started to drive away, I remembered, "I have to call Aunt J and tell her we got a lift." I called her on my cell and hung up to the silence in the car. The evening's events seemed to have drained us of conversation. Francesca stared out the window, a worried frown replacing the expression of exuberance she had shown this evening.

"I'm going to get to the bottom of this fire," Paolo announced, breaking the silence. "I want to know how someone got into the basement to place the fuse device Lt. Red described."

"I never thought of that." I realized that I had just assumed that the house had been broken into for that purpose.

"Wasn't it a break-in?" Francesca could have been reading my mind.

"There was no evidence of a break-in. There's an alarm system anyway."

"I think they came into our basement from the basement next door," Paolo proclaimed.

"Wouldn't the arson investigators have discovered the means of entry?" I asked.

"They say there's no evidence of that. I say they've missed it. There will be no one there tomorrow. Lt. Red told my grandmother that they're finished. He asked her and Max and Frieda to go to police headquarters to make their statements. They'll be having dinner with Uncle Horst after that. I'm going to take the opportunity to see what I can find out for myself." Paolo sounded pleased with himself. "I'm tired of sitting around and watching everyone else try to solve this crime."

"Do you need any help?" Francesca asked. "Annie and I are pretty good at this, you know."

"I don't want to get you into any trouble," he replied.

Francesca laughed. "Hah, don't get me into any trouble. What more can happen to me? I'm already a murder suspect. Jeez, Paolo!"

"And according to Mark DiCristiani, we're living on borrowed time," I added. "I'd like to see the arsonist caught so I can ride the subway again."

"Me too," agreed Francesca. "That was to be the M.O. for our demise, wasn't it, Annie. Mark DiCristiani carries out death by subway."

"Okay! Okay! Count yourselves in," Paolo laughed. "Nothing can happen to us anyway. That's my grandmother's house, not Blue Beard's Castle."

"We'll meet you at your grandma's house, then." Francesca settled it.

"No, there's still a cop guarding the house. I found a back entrance to the house next door. I'll draw you a map. The entrance was unlocked yesterday. I couldn't believe my luck. I hope it's still unlocked. Meet me at six sharp. It's less likely we'll be seen if it's dark."

"This is exciting!" Francesca said. Her mood seemed to lighten at the thought of doing something. Anything!

"You must be a danger addict," I mumbled. I felt a knot of apprehension in my gut. But, Paolo was right. The house next door was empty. There was a cop on the street outside his grandmother's house. Mark DiCristiani didn't dare to show up at that house. He's not that stupid. Finally, I convinced myself that this was a good idea. It wouldn't be the first time we figured things out before the police.

"We arrived home and Paolo drew his little map while Francesca and I stretched and yawned. Six o'clock, tomorrow," he said, kissing us good-bye.

"I had a lovely time, Paolo," smiled Francesca.

"Yes, I did too. We'll have to do it again." He waited until we were safely inside the lobby, then drove off.

"He really likes you, Francesca," I repeated what was so obvious.

"And, I really like him," she chirped.

Inside the apartment there was a note from J: *Thanks for calling about the ride. Got hold of a rollaway bed for F. It's in A's bedroom. Love, J*

Crippled by our high-heeled shoes, we limped into my room and made ready for bed.

We both slept late, Francesca comfortable at last, in a real bed. The phone woke us up. I grabbed it, mumbling a sleepy hello.

It was Aunt J. She wanted to know what our plans were. I told her we had slept late, planned to hang around the apartment and rest, and would meet Paolo at his grandmother's. "We'll probably go out for dinner," I lied.

"I'll send a cab for you, someone I know."

"Aunt J, we'll be okay. We're with Paolo."

"Call when you're ready to come home then. Call by nine, regardless." She added.

"Okay, see you later, Aunt J." I hung up, annoyed at her protective nature, feeling guilty because we were about to do something that would make her very angry.

The afternoon dragged by. I checked my e-mail to see if Ty had sent me a message, just the usual stuff and nothing from Ty.

"I wish we had that little black book," I said.

Francesca was lost in an art text she was using as a source for a research paper.

I thought about my school friends who were skiing and shot off some text messages. It was hard to have to keep all this exciting stuff a secret. At last it was time to leave. I slipped Aunt J's new cell phone into my jeans. For better or worse, we were off.

At six we arrived at our pre-appointed designation. It was dark. We didn't see Paolo until he slid out of the shadows, slapping his arms to keep warm.

"Where's the cop who's guarding this place?" I asked, looking around.

"I've been timing him. It takes him five minutes to make his rounds. He's due to come around that corner in about thirty seconds, so you'd better duck in here with me."

We crouched low, behind the ramp-shaped cellar entrance. Footsteps approached, slowing tentatively. He might have heard our voices. I held my breath. Let's hope he thinks its neighborhood kids. It seemed like forever that he stood there. At last, the footsteps retreated.

My legs cramped suddenly. I stifled a yelp, but fell over with a thump, grazing a garbage can. There was enough of a sound to bring the footsteps to a halt.

Lying on my side, hiding from the cop who was guarding a crime scene, I contemplated Aunt J's reaction if we were discovered. A quick prayer to some unknown guardian angel came to me.

The footsteps continued, and then faded around the corner. We breathed a collective sigh of relief.

"Come. I'll show you the way in." Paolo grabbed Francesca's hand and she mine. In a few seconds we had descended the steps beneath the trap door that we had been hiding behind. The cellar door was unlocked. I found that to be very strange.

My first thought was that I had forgotten to bring a flashlight. I had a cigarette lighter, a Zippo, for emergencies, and a tiny flash light to help find keyholes in the dark. Paolo snapped on a Maglite, making the whole thing easier. We certainly couldn't turn the lights on. Someone could see that the basement had visitors.

The light illuminated the floor of the cellar we had just entered. It was littered with trash, coffee cups and plastic junk, lumber, large rolls of insulation, boxes of nails, and remnants of plywood sheets.

"The first thing we need to figure out is the position of this basement relative to your house," Francesca said.

"Yes. That wall over there is common to our house and this one," he said waving the light over the far wall.

"It's logical that, if there is a link between the two houses, it's over on that wall," I whispered.

"No need to whisper," said Paolo. "No one can hear us down here."

"What's all this stuff on the floor?" I asked.

Paolo shone the light at the floor. Francesca offered, "That's packing material. Like the stuff . . ."

"They ship paintings in," Paolo finished for her.

"I bet that they were going to steal the paintings and get them out of the house by packing them up disguised as building materials," I said. "Between sheets of plywood or in a roll of insulation."

"That's a nice little piece of deduction, Annie. But how were they going to get the paintings out of the vault?" Francesca pointed out.

"That's what we need to find out," Paolo reminded us.

"Yeah, I thought that was why we were here," Francesca quipped, running a hand across the wall, searching with another flashlight produced by Paolo.

"I still don't understand why they set the fire," I said.

"I agree. The charge wasn't enough to blow the safe open," Paolo observed.

"No, no! The charge was just a fuse to start the fire. The purpose was obviously to set a fire, not to blow the safe open," I responded.

"The fire couldn't burn the vault down, so why a fire?" Francesca picked up on the debate.

"Maybe the fire was meant to empty the house out. You know. Make it uninhabitable, so they could have access to the vault." Paolo's voice was muffled as he crouched down to examine the wall with Francesca.

I watched them, thinking of what the cops said. They didn't find a connection between the two basements. If there was arson, investigators had to find a way to go from one house to the other. It must be accessible only from this side.

Paolo made his way along the wall to a section that was made up of sheets of plywood nailed to the studs. He rapped on the wood. It sounded like someone rapping on wood. Francesca, following his example, rapped on the brick wall. She said "Ouch," and sucked on her knuckles. This was going nowhere, except as a script for a Three Stooges movie, or some inane Saturday cartoon show.

Paolo nudged a four-by-four that appeared to be butted up against the wall with his toe. To his surprise, it moved away from the wall. We all looked at it, and approaching the wall carefully, examined the section around the loosened four-by-four. The timber was weighted down on one end with heavy paving stones. We moved the stones and other timbers away from the wall. Paolo picked up a pry bar and started poking and levering at obvious seams and recesses in the wall.

"Look at the floor here," I said. In the light of the Maglite, we could see the parallel scratches leading in an arc, away from the wall. It gave me an idea.

"Could this section of the wall swing in somehow?"

We pushed and pulled. We tested our weight against the wall in every combination we could think of. Finally, the section swung into the basement next door, pivoting on one of the wall beams.

"Hah! So that's why they didn't find the entrance. The wall section swings into the room and there's no way it'll move if this beam and the stones are wedged in place. All the pushing and prying from the other side does nothing."

"Why didn't the police search this basement?" Francesca asked.

"They need a search warrant. For that, they have to show probable cause. They would go for that if all else failed," I said, adding, "Maybe that was the next move."

The smell of the fire was making its way through to our side. "So that's how they got into our basement," Paolo muttered. "But how did they expect to get into the vault?"

"Are you kidding?" snorted Francesca. "With DiCristiani's connections, I'm sure he could find someone to crack a safe, a mere technicality as far as his professional endeavors were concerned."

"No," I said. "The safe combination was on the list of numbers we found taped to DiCristiani's desk drawer, remember? The question is where did he get the combination?"

"Let's put everything back and get out of here before we're caught," Paolo said. "I'm beginning to feel a little nervous about breaking and entering."

The little hairs on the back of my neck were prickling. *He was right.* I was getting jumpy myself. I didn't put up any objections to leaving.

"There's no proof that DiCristiani and Company are behind this, other than his owning the building," I pointed out. "It's unlocked. We got in. Someone else could too."

"Could be why it's left unlocked. It's a good alibi," Paolo said picking up this thread of logic.

"It would be great if we could find something here to connect him to this basement," Francesca stated the obvious.

"DiCristiani was murdered before the fire. Who could have been in this scheme with him to carry on after his death?" Paolo mused.

"What about Mark?" Francesca asked. "He seems very interested in his father's business. He keeps showing up at the gallery. Why would he threaten us the way he did if he didn't have a vested interest in Daddy's business ventures?"

"Annie's right about finding a tangible connection," Paolo said panning his light across the floor. "Just beer and soda cans, a few Styrofoam cups," he observed.

"Anybody got a paper bag?" I asked.

"There on the floor," Francesca pointed. "Aren't you carrying recycling to an extreme?" She quickly added, "Duh, I get it," fingerprints."

"Right, and saliva, and who knows what else the forensics guys will find." Feeling triumphant, I used a tissue to grasp cans and cups, and place them into a bag. A small dark object caught my eye. "Pan the light over here, Paolo," I asked. We all followed Paolo's circle of light. The object was a match book. I picked it up by its edges. There was a phone number on it. I carefully wrapped it in the tissue, and tucked it in my jacket pocket.

"Let's get out of here." We filed towards the exit, finally heeding Paolo's request. As we approached the stairway to the outside, I scanned the floor to see if there were any other items of interest. I walked right into Francesca, pushing her into Paolo.

"What's the prob . . ." My protest was answered as I looked up to see why she wasn't moving. There, at the basement entrance was Mark DiCristiani and the two bad guys who had chased us that first day in the subway.

"Get back inside," Mark hissed, gesturing with a large black pistol, its blunt nose pointed directly at us.

We were almost at the spot. It was a perfect opportunity
for them to shoot us or throw us in the river.

Chapter 14
THE INCIDENT ON THE BRIDGE

I HAD NEVER REALLY LIKED Mark DiCristiani. He was arrogant and too cocky. He acted like Mr. Number One Stud and I didn't like the way he looked at me. Now, all my strong impressions and vague feelings gelled into a tangible thing, I was scared. I started to shake all over. My body wouldn't obey the command to walk. One of the men came down the stairs and pushed me toward the room we had just left.

"I see you snoopy little bitches have been joined by Paolo, here," Mark sneered.

"I don't think I've had the pleasure." Paolo sounded more confident than I could have ever managed.

"I know who you are," Mark continued in his unpleasant tone.

"Then you know I live next door. We're trying to get to the bottom of the fire that was set in our house. Why are you here? What connection do you have with this house?"

I admired Paolo. He was quick on his feet. But his attempt to make us look innocent was in vain.

Mark grabbed the bag of bottles and cans from my hand. "What have we here, Annie Tillery, junior detective?" he asked, voice slashing out at me with sarcasm.

"I can't stand people who don't put their discarded bottles and cans in the recycle bin," I tried, picking up on Paolo's attempt to look innocent. "Nobody cares about this planet," I said, my voice shaking.

"You don't sound too convincing. In fact, you sound like somebody who's been caught in the act," Mark said triumphantly.

"I think you should put the gun down, first of all," Paolo said. "Then let us go on our way. We haven't done anything wrong."

"Breaking and entering is nothing wrong?" Mark sneered.

"Let's let the cops decide," Francesca piped up, joining our defense.

"Shut up!" Mark snarled, throwing our bag of cans and bottle into the corner.

"Tie their hands!" he gestured to his two comrades.

Paolo stepped forward. "What do you think you are doing . . ."

Mark's free hand swung out and his closed fist caught Paolo across the bridge of the nose. Paolo was on the floor before he could finish his protest.

Francesca gasped next to me. I felt frozen. "What are you going to do with us?" I asked my voice as steady as I could make it.

"We're going to take a little walk over the Brooklyn Bridge," he advised us with a note of glee in his voice. "You and your friends are going to party here in the basement; a little cocaine, a little marijuana, a little vodka, and then you're going to the bridge for a nice flying lesson. You like adventure, right?"

Mark turned to the other two who had finished tying Francesca's hands and were now coming to me. "Leave the usual evidence for a case of accidental drug overdose. Okay gentlemen?" He laughed. It was an ugly sound.

Francesca tried to get to the stairs, panic finally taking over her already stressed mind. One of the thugs grabbed her arm and shoved her back into the basement. They were taping my hands together. An inane thought crossed my mind, high tech criminals, these guys. They didn't use rope. They had graduated to duct tape, much stronger. No knot to undo, definitely a superior choice. My mind seemed to be going elsewhere.

"What time is it?" I asked, not knowing what difference it could make.

"It's too late for the three of you," Mark gloated.

"You won't get away with murdering the three of us, Mark," I said, feeling dizzy from the desperation that had landed on me. I was supposed to call Aunt J at nine. Was it close to nine?

"They'll never find the bodies, Annie Tillery," he snarled. "You ever see the current in the East River? You'll be swept out to sea in a couple of hours."

"You can't just kill us!" I protested, starting to lose control.

He looked at me and laughed. "Oh, but I can. It's not that hard to kill."

Was this a confession? I looked at his face. His eyes were dark and flat, like the coins they put over dead peoples' eyes in Viking movies. I thought he must have killed his father. If he could do that, he could kill anyone. Hope spiraled down into a black abyss. I thought desperately for something to say, to derail him from his plan.

Paolo was leaning against the wall, having struggled to his feet, blood caking in two dark streaks on his upper lip. Hatred darted from his eyes as he watched Mark. Francesca appeared not to be breathing, pale and shaking like a leaf.

In the fog of disbelief that engulfed me, I heard a hail of small objects hit the floor. One bounced near the toe of my boot, a crack vial, a few little plastic envelopes, some rolling papers and last of all, the clinking of a vodka bottle rolling across the floor. Mark pulled Francesca's scarf off, and tossed it in the corner. The evidence had been planted.

"Let's go," Mark commanded flatly.

The cop on patrol, I thought. I looked at Francesca and Paolo, wondering if they remembered. If we could make noise, he would . . .

Mark's short assistant was rolling a rug out on the floor. He pushed Paolo down on it, slapping a piece of tape across his mouth. He rolled Paolo up in the rug, and then they packaged Francesca and me. I forgot about the patrol cop. I had a new problem, making sure I could breathe.

I wondered in despair, if the cop on patrol would even remember seeing three oriental rugs being removed from the brownstone next door once the investigation of our murders got under way. We were being placed in a van. I figured it was a van from the sound the door made as it slammed shut. The dust from the rug filled my nose and I concentrated on just getting enough oxygen.

We rode for only a short time before the van stopped. I felt waves of vertigo as my rug-home was hoisted in the air. We bounced along for a while. There was a nauseating fall and I hit the floor with a jarring thud. I could barely make out the sounds outside my woolly prison. I felt, more than heard, two thuds nearby.

There was stillness for a time. I strained to hear. Nothing. Panic rose in me. I began to struggle. If this was the end I wasn't going without a fight. I lurched, first to one side, then the other. At last, I rolled out of the rug, snorting great drafts of air through my nose.

We were in a warehouse. It was brightly lit. Francesco and Paolo were beginning to roll out as I had done. I watched them intently, willing them out, unable to help them in any other way.

So engrossed was I that I failed to hear the approaching footsteps. A rough hand grabbed my head, ripping the tape from my mouth. The same was happening to my friends. Oh, thank God, I thought fleetingly, before I saw what was to happen next. The smell hit me just before I saw and felt the rag that was clamped over my face. The hand with the rag had a light sprinkling of blond hairs and a large gold ring. Then, nothingness!

****

"Stop snoring," I demanded, indignantly. *Who is snoring in my bed?* I opened my eyes to see. Lights of incredible intensity stabbed at my eyes. Letters began to come into focus. *DiCristiani Industries*, a stenciled sign on the door declared. Nausea crept up my throat. We must be in DiCristiani's warehouse. I tried to hold my head. Why couldn't I move my hands?

Memory pushed its foot down on the accelerator nerve of my heart. I looked around. Francesca and Paolo were still out, snoring. We were still in the same spot as before. I heard footsteps coming, and quickly closed my eyes pretending to be asleep like the others.

"They're still out. Is it time now?" one of them said.

"Yeah, I want to get this over with. Wake them," Mark ordered.

The three of us got wake up calls in the form of a boot in the butt. "I have to go to the bathroom," I announced. Anything to stall for time and to try to grab an opportunity to escape.

"Me too," said Francesca in a groggy voice.

The two men looked at Mark. "Why not?" He shrugged.

"You've got to take the tape off my hands."

Again the men looked at Mark. He nodded. "Lock them in, one at a time. What can they do in there? Flush themselves down the john?" He laughed at his own attempt at humor.

I couldn't believe our luck. Another one of his endearing traits, Mark was so arrogant and so sure he had us that he was getting sloppy. This was the only chance I had to do something, but what?

That's it! I thought. *The cell phone! The one J had given us. God! I hope it didn't fall out of my pocket.* The knock-out stuff they used to put us to sleep ruined my ability to act quickly and in a coordinated fashion.

Just as I slipped my hands in my jean pocket, searching for the 7 button, Mark looked over at me and saw my hand fumbling in my pocket. He lurched at me grabbing for my arm. My finger pressed and held as he pulled at my arm, viciously wrenching it up as he rammed my elbow into the wall to make me let go.

Mark threw the cell against the wall where it fell in three pieces. I could only hope I had pressed the 7 long enough to send the signal. Clutching my arm I said, "Let me use the lav. I'm going to be sick." I sounded much stronger than I felt.

One of the thugs pushed me into the small lav near what appeared to be an office. I leaned against the sink trying to shake off the nausea and willing myself not to cry. *Think! Think! What else can I do?*

"C'mon, hurry up. Don't make me come in and get you." I could hear the lurid smirk in the voice outside.

All I could think to do was to leave a note somewhere in the bathroom where it might be found. After all, it was DiCristiani's warehouse. It would be searched. At least J would know what happened to us.

There was a lot of graffiti on the bathroom walls. I fished in my jacket pocket and found a lipstick, another example of Mark and Company's sloppiness. *He just doesn't give a girl credit for how inventive she can be with a lipstick.* I thought. To the rest of the messages by the sink, I added my own.

I used symbols for my and Aunt J's initials and added, 2/18, THE LAST NITE. The symbols were a code we had agreed on as a signal for identifying each other in a game I played with J when I was about ten. I hoped they would jump out at her if she ever came here to search with the Crime Scene Unit. I wiped away the tears that welled up in my eyes and knocked to be let out. As Francesca went in, I saw the lipstick case on the sink. I had forgotten it! If it were possible to feel any more desperate, I would have. If our captors checked and saw the lipstick, they might match the color to my graffiti and that would be the end of that plan.

I was taped again. Paolo returned with the other thug and was taped. Francesca knocked and was let out. Before the door shut, I tried to see if the lipstick was still there. It was gone! I looked at Francesca. She already had tape across her mouth and was trying not to sob. Paolo stood stiffly by.

They led us out to the van at gun point. It was completely deserted outside. Looking around for any form of assistance, I saw the big white digital numbers of a bank clock. It read 3:29AM. We had been asleep for a long time. That must have been the idea. Wait until there would be no chance of a passerby on the bridge. No witnesses.

They pushed us into the back of the van, onto the floor. Mark drove, the others sat above us with a foot in the small of our backs, guns pointed at our heads. In a mercifully short time the van stopped and they pulled us out. I recognized Cadman Plaza, the Brooklyn side of the bridge.

"We're going to un-tape you now. If you run, I'll shoot you. No one will come. They'll think the noise is a truck backfiring." Mark delivered his lovely little speech in a completely business-like way. I knew what he said was true because this was one of the busiest truck roads in New York City.

"You killed your own father," I said tasting the blood on my torn lips. I didn't care anymore what I said to him. I knew what I was going to do when we got up on the bridge. I was going to make a run for it. I had nothing to lose. The angrier he was, the worse his decisions would be. Somehow, when the time came, I would figure out a way to signal Francesca and Paolo. Right now, I would goad Mark. Maybe he'd shoot his own nose off.

"Are they teaching you how to get away with murder in law school, DiCristiani? You're just a common criminal with not much on the ball. You blew the arson job. You couldn't come up with a more creative way of dealing with us, you know, one that would keep you off death row."

All the time I spoke, he moved closer to me, the gun leveled at my head. He held it in one hand. This gave me confidence that I wasn't about to be shot.

Aunt J had taken me to the firing range often, and I'd used a hand gun enough times to know when someone is serious about shooting you with a pistol, they hold the gun with two hands. If, and I doubted this, he had no experience with pistols and he fired one-handed, the shot would not hit me, except at point-blank range, which he was fast approaching. I went to duck. His free hand lashed out and slapped me hard across the face. I tasted more blood.

"No marks, Mr. D. No marks," the short thug admonished. "This is supposed to be an accidental death." He regained control.

They marched us onto the path leading to the stairs that took us up to the pedestrian walk-way. We went single-file, one captor ahead of us, Mark and the short thug behind us. An occasional car whizzed by in the traffic lane which would end up below us as we moved toward the center of the bridge. It got windier near center span. I tried something. "Francesca, can you hear me?"

"Yes. Keep talking. I don't think they can hear you."

"Ask Paolo if he can hear you." A short silence followed. I couldn't hear them if they were talking. That meant that our captors couldn't hear us either. The wind and traffic noises were in our favor. As long as we didn't turn our heads, or make gestures, we might get away with it.

"Yeah, he can hear me. Annie, I'm going to make a run for it when the time comes. We all should. They can't get all of us. If we're lucky they won't get any of us."

"What's Paolo going to do?" I asked. Another silence followed.

"The same," she answered simply.

I looked ahead. We were approaching the first pier, where the walkway went around a massive support pier. You couldn't see the path ahead. This was the point where you were least likely to be seen by a passing car. That's where they would try to push us over.

"I think they'll make their move up by that pier," I said to Francesca. "Tell Paolo."

In a few seconds she replied: "It's a go."

I hoped that they would be somewhat distracted, observing traffic, trying to pick the right moment. Three of them, three of us. Paolo had the best chance to get away. He was the farthest away from most of them.

We were almost at the spot. The walkway widened. It was a perfect opportunity for them to grab us and dump us into the frigid water; but also, the worst opportunity to shoot us.

Out of the side of my eye, I saw their plan in an instant. Mark turned his gun exclusively on Paolo. He was going to be the hardest one to throw over the rail. They'd take care of him first. We were at the pier now. This was it. The lead thug turned to me. I knew this was my time to run.

What I saw happening in front of me made all flight unnecessary. A cyclist, going at top speed, came around from the other side of the pier. He hit my attacker square in the back, spilling onto the ground himself. I jumped aside and for the moment, I was saved. I turned to run. Short thug was about to shoot Francesca. She was running back towards Brooklyn. Her assailant didn't see me. I wasn't close enough to tackle him. I needed something to throw. The cyclist's water bottle obliged, by rolling toward me. I grabbed it, and whaled it at him. It made a thunking noise as it hit him directly on his ugly head. He went down on his knees, stunned.

I caught up with Francesca. "Where's Paolo?" I cried. She pointed. On the walkway, up ahead, Paolo was sprawled on the ground. Mark was standing over him, gun aimed at his head. "Nooo!" I screamed.

Mark turned towards us like a deer caught in a car's headlights. He hadn't seen what had happened at the pier, with the cyclist. He must have thought that we were already in the water. Behind Mark, a form approached us, indistinguishable at first. It moved fast. Mark turned his gun back to Paolo.

The new arrival shot at Mark, winging his hand with the gun. Mark rolled to the edge of the walkway and dropped to the roadway below. The figure came into full view. It was Horst Blau!

Francesca gasped. I started to run toward him. He'd saved us. "Help us!" I cried. He raised the gun, aiming it straight at me. "No! It's me, Anne Tillery." Why was he aiming the gun at me? My mind couldn't grasp what I saw. I could hear Francesca running close behind me. Before I could warn her, I went sprawling to the ground, Francesca on top of me. The last thing I saw before the pavement was the blast from Horst's gun. The bullet pinged off the bridge's steel-work. I still couldn't figure it out. Why was Horst shooting at us?

Francesca held my head down. "He's that man from the hallway in DiCristiani's apartment house. The one I saw when I found the body," she breathed in my ear. "The ring. I remembered the ring. But also, his hand. The ring and the hand!"

It took a few seconds for everything to make sense. We were facing DiCristiani's killer, who would in turn, kill all of us. My body tensed, waiting for the next bullet to ring out. Then I heard a different sound. The squalling of a police siren grew louder and louder as we lay frozen, in the early hours of a New York morning.

Chapter 15
THE MURDERER

THE BULLET NEVER CAME. FRANCESCA rolled off of me as I struggled to turn my head in the direction of Horst. He was gone. Mark DiCristiani was gone.

"Paolo! Where's Paolo?" I croaked, barely able to talk. We stumbled back toward the pier. The thug who'd been hit by the cyclist was lying on the path, groaning. His buddy was nowhere in sight.

The police siren had switched to a whoop-whoop melody as the cruiser pulled to a stop. The lights atop the patrol car washed the scene in a flashing glare of red white and blue lights. At another time I might enjoy the resemblance to a TV shoot for C.S.I., N.Y.

The cyclist came from around the corner, and trotted over to the police officer as he emerged from the car.

"Where's Paolo?" Francesca was sobbing, breath ragged.

"Did you see another guy around?" I yelled. "He was with us, not running away with the bad guys."

"He's down on the roadway. He hurt his leg when he fell. Also, he seems to have an injured arm." The cyclist looked at us strangely and then turned to talk to the policeman who had run over from one of the wailing patrol cars. "I'm the one who called 911," he explained. "I think I really hurt that guy over there. I train at this time of the morning to avoid this kind of thing. At first I thought this was a simple accident, but I did witness some gunfire and these people seem to be in some kind of trouble."

Another cruiser and an ambulance pulled up to add to the din. The police officer looked at Francesca and me, then turned to the cyclist. "Sir, you still have to give a statement to my partner in the patrol car." He gestured to one of the police cars.

"Ladies, can you tell me what happened? I received a call from Detective Tillery. She said that she received a cellphone message from you, an extreme emergency. The last GPS signal from the cell located you in a warehouse not far from here. I was on my way when . . ." He swung his arm in an arc to encompass the scene around us and then continued, "I came across this." He turned to give us a quizzical look. "So, what gives here, girls?"

"We were kidnapped," I started, breathing hard, trying to grasp that we had just escaped a dive into the icy waters of the East River. "They were going to throw us off the bridge," I continued, cutting to the chase. "Can we see if our friend is okay?"

The patrolman yelled to the ambulance crew on the roadway below. "What's the status of the guy with the leg injury?"

One of the EMT's climbed to the pedestrian walk and reported on Paolo's condition. "Leg's broken. Bullet wound to the arm. Missed the bone. We got him stabilized. He was going into shock."

"Can we see him?" I asked.

"No. I need you here," the officer replied.

The EMT looked at us. "You two don't look too good either," he observed.

The patrolman said, "What hospital?"

"Bellevue." The EMT guy started to leave. Francesca grabbed his arm. "Tell the guy with the broken leg that Annie and Francesca are okay, please."

"Will do." He was gone.

"I need to get your story so we don't miss anything here. Then you can join your friend in the ER."

"I need to call my aunt," I said, contemplating Aunt J's reaction to what we had just gotten into.

"From the hospital," he shot back. "I already radioed your location." He continued what seemed to me to be relentless questioning.

We repeated what we had told him.

"Where's the van again?"

We gave him the exact location. I even had its license number. I had memorized it before our walk on the bridge.

Francesca suddenly sat down, sobbing. I didn't need much motivation to do the same, but the cold cut through my clothes and the shivering was all I could concentrate on. Mr.

Humane, the police officer, was staring at us, trying to decide what to do with us when the second EMT vehicle arrived.

"You finished with them?" one of them asked.

"I'm not finished questioning them yet. I have to secure a crime scene."

I snapped. Whether it was the cold or the horror of the last few hours, this was the last straw. I shot out at him, "Do the whole freakin' bridge!" Looking up at him sullenly, I said, "You know, all possible points of entry and egress." Another one of Aunt J's lessons.

"These girls are going into shock and hypothermia, so get your information fast, if you want it at all," said the other EMT in a serious tone.

"You're supposed to be helping us, not killing us. That was the other guys. I'm getting into the ambulance," I said, pulling Francesca to her feet. She slumped against me and if the EMT hadn't caught me, we both would have gone down. Our interrogator finally agreed to continue the questioning at the hospital. The last I saw of the bridge was the crime scene van approaching, a vehicle alone on a bridge that had been cordoned off by a covey of police vehicles.

"What happened to your mouth?" the female EMT asked.

"Someone used us as a demo for the durability of duct tape." I felt so giddy. There was little sensation in my limbs.

"Drink this," she said as they wrapped us in warm blankets. "The report says that you were kidnapped. Were you raped as well?" Her tone was gentle.

Ugh I thought. I squeezed my eyes shut to block such an image. "No. We just knew too much about those guys. They wanted us out of the way."

She gave us a quizzical look.

We arrived at the hospital. Feeling was returning to my limbs in painful pins and needles.

"Can you walk?" I was asked. I got up, but the pain in my thawing legs was too much. Francesca appeared to be asleep. She was carried in on a stretcher. I got the wheel chair.

Inside the ER, there was a female police officer. "I have to call my aunt," I said, looking at her with all the fierceness I could muster, "Detective Jill Tillery," emphasis on the detective, "326-0290." After this caper I was sure I would never see life outside of our apartment or school.

A nurse came over, "We're admitting you for observation."

"No, you're not!" I blurted out, sobbing. "You . . ."

She didn't let me finish. "Go ahead, get up and leave."

I knew she was right. Besides, I wouldn't get past the cops. "What happened to my friend, Paolo, the guy with the broken leg and gun shot wound in the arm?" It was so hard to get the shaking and sobbing under control enough to talk coherently.

"He's stable, but they took him up to surgery. The leg break is a bad one. They'll have to put a steel pin in it."

They put Francesca and me in beds in the ER. I must have fallen asleep because the next thing I knew, Aunt J was standing over me shaking my shoulder.

"I want you to know, Annie, I do love you so much, but right now, my gratitude that you and your friends are alive is being quickly superseded by the need to make you understand how angry I am at your foolishness. I am at a loss as to how to keep your snoopy little nose out of trouble." Her face was white, her lips tightly drawn over her teeth as she spoke, barely controlling herself.

"Yes, Aunt J," was all I dared to say. She looked like an angel to me, even if she was an avenging angel.

"I'm taking you home tonight and locking both of you up and throwing away the key." The nurse came in and Aunt J signed the release papers.

With her help, and the ever-faithful Lt. Red, we limped out of the hospital into the dawning light of a new day I thought I would never see.

Later that day, we headed downtown to police headquarters. I hoped that this was the last time. The detectives assigned to the case questioned us, taking our statements. They needed descriptions and identifications.

"Am I still a suspect, after all this?" Francesca asked in a tired voice.

"No, there wasn't time to tell you. Your DNA fingerprint didn't match the crime scene evidence."

"So, whose blood is it?" I asked.

"We don't know. The forensics team will have to take blood from all your playmates from last night."

"Are they in jail?" Francesca asked.

"Except for the one the cyclist got last night, they all got away," Aunt J reported. "The one in the hospital is in serious condition with a broken back. He hasn't been too talkative."

"Mark DiCristiani got away?" Francesca sounded deflated. "I can't believe it. He won't stop until he gets us. You'll see." She seemed to shrink into herself there in the back seat, resignation written all over her.

"You won't feel so frightened once you get some real rest," Aunt J said in a comforting voice.

"I'm so glad I gave you that phone. It worked, you know," she continued.

"Yes, the policeman at the bridge told us he had our location from the phone's GPS. If you only knew how close it came to not working." I told her how I got to push the 7 even though our hands had been tied most of the time.

"Don't worry," Aunt J said confidently. "We'll get Mark and the other guy."

"Horst Blau, too?" Francesca asked, ignoring her cheerful confidence.

"Maybe they'll kill each other and we won't have to worry about either of them," I speculated, Francesca's gloominess creeping into my bones.

"The police, FBI and Interpol are searching," Aunt J responded with resolve. "Kidnapping is a federal crime and Horst is not an American citizen."

At headquarters we were introduced to the detective handling the case, Detective Mills. I made sure to tell him about the clues we had left behind for them the night before. "There's a bag of bottles in the basement of the house next door to Frau Helriegel's. We put them in the bag because we thought they might contain fingerprints."

"Did anyone touch them after you put them in the bag?" Detective Mills asked. "No," I replied. I remembered the matchbook and fished in my pocket for it, turning it over to Detective Mills.

"There's a note written in lipstick on the bathroom wall in the warehouse," I added, writing out a facsimile of the note for him.

"Do you have the lipstick?" he asked. Francesca dug it out of her jacket pocket. "Good. We can run a chromatography on this and the lipstick on the wall to show a match. Your fingerprints should be there as well. This will be important evidence in the kidnapping trial."

"Miss Tillery, can you tell us anything about the gun that Mark DiCristiani had? We found some ballistic evidence at the crime scene on the bridge. It could be helpful."

I laughed "Yes. Actually, I know the make. It's common, a Smith and Wesson 9mm." He looked at me strangely. "I had to do a paper on gun control for social studies last year," I offered. He seemed relieved at this logical explanation for my knowledge of firearms. I suppressed the urge to tell him that it was the piece I carried on the subway.

"There was no gun at the bridge scene, but we did recover bullets. Knowing the type of firearm is going to make the job easier for the people in ballistics. We can also run a check to see if it's registered," he added. "You said Horst Blau aimed his gun straight at you. Do you remember anything about that gun?"

I put my head in my hands, closing my eyes, trying to recapture that confusing moment. Visualizing the hands with the gun, I told him, "It was a large gun, a Magnum, or some sort of semi-automatic." I looked up. "Francesca tackled me and said it was the man from the apartment house." I added this, remembering the ring. Our interrogator looked confused.

I turned to Francesca. "When you made the sketch of the man you saw in the apartment house, you tried to remember the ring."

"Yes," Francesca replied, concentrating on Detective Mills. "I kept trying to remember what was on the ring. I thought it was an initial, but I wasn't sure. Then, at the lecture, I noticed that Mr. Blau had a ring on and something kept nagging at me. I didn't connect the two until last night, on the bridge. I saw the ring again. But it was the combination of the ring and his hand that helped me remember, and it all clicked. When I saw him at the lecture I never got a clear picture of the ring on the hand. He gestured with his hands a lot, or had them in his pockets."

Frowning down at his pad, Detective Mills said, "Let me get this straight, the day DiCristiani was murdered, you saw a man coming down the stairs as you were going up. You noticed a ring on his hand and then recognized this ring on the hand of Horst Blau when you saw him on the bridge."

"Not entirely accurate. It was seeing the ring on the hand. He was very close to me when he popped up on the bridge. There was plenty of light on that part of the bridge. That's how I could see it so clearly," Francesca nodded adamantly.

"Did you see the ring in detail either of those times?" he pressed.

"Not in detail," she answered. "Only that it was large, like a signet ring. Paolo had one just like it."

"You said that the initial had all straight lines," I added.

"Yes, like an H," Francesca said, eyes triumphant.

"Francesca, do you still have the sketch you made of the mystery man?" I asked.

"Yes."

Detective Mills eyes lit up. "Can you bring it to us?" We have a new program for our computer that helps us create sketches of suspects and compare them to the photographs of suspects."

"Yes," she said again, but appeared distracted. "Do you think you'll ever find Mark DiCristiani or Horst Blau?" Francesca couldn't hide the fear in her voice.

Detective Mills picked up the phone and checked with another officer who told him that the surveillance detail assigned to Mark's apartment had only reported a neighbor's story that he had shown up there around four this morning and left fifteen minutes later.

"We're checking everything, even the private air traffic out of here." With that statement, our interview came to a conclusion. Detective Mills told us to send in the sketch and he gave us a fax number. "This is my pager number. If you remember anything else or you need to contact me for anything, that's the way to do it."

Aunt J met us and we left. "While you were being interviewed, I called the hospital to check on Paolo. Would you like to see him?"

Francesca brightened for the first time all day. "Yes, I'd feel so much better if I could see him."

"Yes!" I echoed enthusiastically.

The investigation, according to Aunt J, had found that Horst Blau had been able to cover any illegal activities and connections quite effectively. He had also dropped off the radar.

"He'll have to surface eventually though, to get money," Francesca observed, turning at last from her brooding appraisal of the passing scenery.

"If he had a secret collection of stolen art, and if he had connections to a man like DiCristiani, he could also have sources of funds under aliases. He certainly had the resources to do that," Aunt J pointed out.

"After what Frau Helriegel told us, there's no telling how many lives Horst Blau leads," I mused.

"If anyone could go underground and not be found, Horst Blau has the where-with-all to do it," Aunt J agreed. "It's a different story with Mark," she went on. "He doesn't have the resources to disappear. He's the one who'll eventually have to surface to get money."

"You don't think he'll just take a one of those big freighters and work his way around the world?" I asked.

"He's a spoiled brat, Annie. Real work is not an option because he has no idea what it is." Francesca offered her insight into Mark's psyche.

"And when he surfaces, I don't want him to find the two of you," Aunt J said solemnly, pulling into a parking space in front of the hospital.

Chapter 16
Mark Pays a Visit

Paolo was making a good recovery. The physical therapist was working with him as we entered the room.

"This inflatable cast will allow you a great deal more mobility than you think," said the therapist. "We've done enough for today. I'll leave you to your visitors. See you tomorrow." She smiled at us and left.

"I can't believe it! I'm going home tomorrow," Paolo exclaimed. "The bullet wound was only superficial, so I can use my crutches."

"How is your grandmother taking all of this?" J asked.

"She is an amazing woman. She told me she was grateful I wasn't killed. That was the important thing to her." Paolo's smile turned to a grimace as he tried to sit down on the edge of the bed.

As we helped him, he confided in us, "It's Uncle Horst who has me upset. He was going to shoot you. It makes me wonder if he would have killed me too." His voice cracked.

"Paolo, your uncle shot at Mark DiCristiani, which saved your life when Mark was ready to blow your head off!" Francesca exclaimed.

Trying to move away from the discomfort of the moment, I asked Paolo, "Can you tell us about your uncle's ring?"

"Yes, if you mean the one he wears all the time, the signet ring with his initial on it?"

"That's the one," prompted Francesca.

"It was a gift from his father. That's why he always wears it. They were very close. The one I have is, as you know, a gift from him."

Francesca and I looked at each other.

"What?" Paolo looked at us impatiently.

"The man I saw coming down from DiCristiani's apartment the day I found him had a ring on just like that. I believe it was your uncle."

"We think he killed John DiCristiani because he was selling forgeries to the secret circle of art collectors," Aunt J added. "We also believe that he followed Mark DiCristiani and company to the brownstone. He must have seen what was going on and decided to tail you all to the bridge. It was a splendid opportunity to get rid of all of you. You knew too much."

"I wonder if he was afraid of what else an investigation of him might find," I asked.

Paolo looked crushed. "I feel so betrayed," he whispered. "I thought we were very close too. I was so proud of him."

"You need to concentrate on getting better," Francesca urged him. "His actions are no reflection on you," she added.

"Will you miss the next semester because of your injury?" I asked.

"I hope not," he said quietly. Brightening, he added, "Come and visit me tomorrow. We'll celebrate our survival."

"We'll come after the gallery," Francesca promised, looking to me for my assent. "It's Friday, and I must prepare for the art classes, as well as receive a shipment of paintings that we're expecting."

Francesca approached the bed. "I'm glad you're okay, Paolo. You could've been killed." Her voice wavered, but she went on, "I was so scared."

"We could've all been killed," he said hugging her.

I looked at Aunt J. Her lips were drawn together in a hard line. She hugged me, then held me at arm's length and shook her head. I could barely hold on to my tears and the awful shaking came back.

We all kissed Paolo good-bye and left. Francesca and I hit the bed and slept until the next morning.

Friday was spent hard at work at the gallery. Francesca had developed a filing system and I sorted the mail while she attended to the shipment of paintings, cataloguing the new acquisitions.

Deeply engrossed in our work, both Francesca and I jumped when my cell rang. I retrieved it from my coat pocket. It was Aunt J. She explained that the police officer who was assigned to us had been called to an emergency in Central Park, but that she had a new officer assigned to us. He would arrive in a half hour. She gave his name as Frank Caputo and filled me in with a brief description.

"Annie, are all the doors locked?"

"Yes, Aunt J. I'll check again though."

We hung up and I slipped the phone back into my coat pocket. We went back to work, anxious to get out of the gallery.

"I wonder whose blood that was at DiCristiani's apartment," Francesca mused.

"It could have been Horst's. He might have cut himself somehow," I speculated.

"It could have been Mark's also," Francesca added. "If it was, it doesn't prove anything. He had every right to be there."

"It could have been old blood," I said. "Anyone who was there for any reason could have left it."

"Can they do a DNA fingerprint on old blood?" Francesca wanted to know.

"Sure. They've done mummies' blood samples," I responded.

"Have they done daddies' blood samples too?" Francesca asked, not showing much humor.

I looked up at her, noting her faraway look. "Francesca! You've been cleared! But you seem so glum. Why?"

"I know. I feel guilty about it. I've got a new job, my wonderful Paolo. You've all been so good to me and I just can't snap out of it." She shook her head, "It's Mark, and I'm scared. I just can't shake the feeling that he'll come back for us, Annie. There's a screw loose there in my opinion."

"I also think he's pretty stupid," I said. "He took a big chance trying to kill us, because there really wasn't any strong evidence against him. He didn't kill his father, so there wouldn't be any murder charge. The evidence for the arson was shaky. The door to the house was unlocked. A good lawyer would point out that anyone could have started the fire. He could have claimed that he didn't know anything about his father's art scam."

"He must have been afraid that if he were investigated, the police would find something incriminating," Francesca concluded.

"Why didn't Mark go after Horst? He's the one who killed his father."

"We know that now. Did Mark know that?" Francesca wondered. "Mark could be afraid of Horst. His father was a big man in the mob. If Horst could kill him, he must be tough, in the eyes of Mark and his gang."

"What about Frau Helriegel?" Francesca asked, continuing her run down of the main characters.

"What about her?" I responded.

"I wonder if she knew that Horst was going to kill John DiCristiani?"

"I don't know. I don't think she'd own up to it if she did. The only charges against her are buying stolen art pieces. She'd be crazy to admit to knowing about this murder. I even doubt, at her age, that she'll ever serve jail time for the procurement of stolen art treasures. The judge could decide that she needs to pay a big fine and support a public service program."

"Do you think all those people on the list will have to give back their paintings?"

I stopped filing and turned to her. "Francesca, if they can't find the paintings because they're in an underground crypt, or vault, or cave, or on the moon somewhere, how can they be asked to give the paintings back, no less be charged with theft?" As I said it, I realized that we had just scratched the surface of what could be a huge cache of stolen art and forgeries. "I think it highly unlikely that any of these treasures will be found, and that justice will be done by charging these people, or returning the art to the rightful owners."

"How many art dealers do you think died in the attempt to stiff these people with fakes?" Francesca snorted.

"Now, there's a thought," I said, considering this latest idea. "This gets more involved all the time. Just when we think we've tied up all the loose ends, another strand pops loose."

I continued, "Even proving Horst guilty of the murder of John DiCristiani is not a sure thing. No one has ever traced the gun at the crime scene to him. The blood has also not been traced to him, and unless he shows up to give a sample, it never will."

"Only my recognizing him as the man who was leaving DiCristiani's apartment has pointed a finger at him."

"That's not enough," I asserted. "It only puts him in the building, not even in the apartment. Just because he was in the building doesn't make him the murderer. For the same reason it didn't make you the murderer."

"His trying to murder us, and then disappearing, is the most incriminating thing against him, I guess," Francesca observed. "When things went bad for him on the bridge, he could have said he didn't recognize us, and that he was trying to help Paolo, or something," she continued.

"No. It was too risky. Aunt J is right. He has the resources to just disappear and live happily ever after."

The phone rang. It was Paolo.

"You're bored, huh?" I heard Francesca say.

"Sure. We can close up here and be at your place in about a half hour," she continued. "Good-bye," Francesca placed the phone in its cradle and said, "Paolo wants us to come to dinner. Frieda and Max made a pot roast and a little celebration for us. What say we finish up here and head over there?"

"Sounds good to me, I'm hungry."

Francesca laughed. "You're always hungry."

I tidied up my filing while Francesca tied up all the packing materials for the trash collectors. "I'm going to check the conservatory," I said. "To make sure everything is ready for tomorrow's lesson."

"Good idea," she mumbled, fishing around in the planter.

"What are you doing?" I asked.

"Looking for the . . . Ah, here it is, the black book. We still haven't looked at it."

"Let's take it with us. We can go through it tonight with Paolo," I added, thinking what a busy night we were about to have. I needed to make sure everything was secure.

It was already dark and no lights were on in the conservatory at the end of the hall. My skin crawled a little at the thought of having to walk that distance in the dark. "Nerves," I said, shaking myself. I made it down the hall.

As I stepped into the conservatory, I heard a soft click, the sound a latch makes when closing, or opening. I flicked on the lights, Nothing! Everything was as I had left it. Perfect. No. One easel had fallen over. As I righted it, I heard a thud back in the office and a muffled sound that I could not identify. My heart beat pounded in my ears.

"Francesca!" I yelled. No answer. My knees felt weak. "It's nothing," I muttered. I walked quickly out of the conservatory, snapped off the lights and hurried down the hall toward the office. Francesca already had the lights off. I thought, *Boy, she's in a hurry.* Only the foyer lights were on.

"You're not . . ." The words were cut off as I was grabbed, my arm twisted behind me.

"Not a sound!" It was Mark DiCristiani. Francesca was right. He had come back and he had his gun. At least he was alone this time.

"What did you come back for?" I asked, immediately wondering why I asked such a stupid question. "This place is being watched," I added. "You'll never get away this time."

"Nice try," he said. "You just never give up being smart, do you?"

"Where's Francesca?" I demanded.

"Out cold on the floor. I need to ask you some questions." I guessed he couldn't risk having the two of us conscious at the same time.

"Where are the keys to this place?" He snapped on the lights. I had to stall him. It was already fifteen minutes since Paolo called. He expected us in another fifteen. How long would it take him to wonder what happened to us, and call up the marines? The special phone was shattered.

"There are a lot of keys for different things," I said, "What keys are you looking for?"

"I want to look at all the keys. Tell me where they are," he demanded, menacing me with the pistol.

"Open the bottom desk door," I directed, "there are some hanging on that door, also in the desk drawer. I'm going to help Francesca," I said. Her inert body alarmed me.

"Stay right there, where I can see you," he motioned at me. "It doesn't matter how she's doing."

"There are keys in the back kitchen too," I said, hoping to stall for time. Warming to the technique, I added, "We haven't finished reorganizing the office. There could be more keys that we haven't found yet."

Francesca groaned.

"Go over there and sit on the floor next to her, and no tricks!"

I went over to Francesca. Blood trickled from a scalp wound. On an impulse, I looked up at Mark and asked, "How did you know about the vault in Frau Helriegel's basement?"

He chuckled, pulling the keys off the hooks on the door. He looked at each, tossing them on the desk. His eyes darted from the keys to us. *He must be looking for some specific key,* I thought

"It was easy once we decided she had to have some place to store her paintings. She bought stuff that was hot. She had to keep it hidden. My father got very curious and when he saw the FOR SALE sign on the house next door, he decided to make a move."

"So, he just bought the house? Not knowing? What if she kept the paintings in Germany?" I had to keep the conversation going. I sensed a certain pride he felt, having discovered the vault. I hoped he would want to talk about it. It also slowed the process of finding the key he was looking for.

He fell for it. "My father had a lot of connections. He checked out her real estate holdings. The Brooklyn house was the only property she owned."

"But how did buying the house next door help you to find the vault?" I pictured Mark, his father, and the two thugs spending endless hours rapping on walls, counting bricks, drilling holes, trying to find the vault.

Mark was frustrated. The door did not hold the key he was looking for. He started to go through the keys in the drawer in the same methodical way. "We knew there was a vault because we got the house plans from some minor bureaucrat in the County Seat. My father greased his palm, and presto, we had the blueprints. After that, it was a matter of making measurements. We needed to break in, so we made it look like we were renovating the house. This was a good front for drilling and sawing our way through to the basement. We watched the house. One day, when they all went out, we went in and measured. We matched the measurements up with the blueprints. That located the vault."

"How did you get the combination?"

"More bribes! Everyone has a price. We had to be careful though, not to be too pushy, in case somebody sounded the alarm on us."

"Why the fire?" Francesca asked, having come back to the land of the living.

"Now you two are so smart. Can't you figure that one out?" he sneered. "We needed to get everyone out of the house for a long period of time. The fire would do that. It didn't work the way we expected, because the old couple wasn't supposed to be there. Had the fire gone on longer, there would have been enough damage to make the house uninhabitable and to destroy the arson evidence. We could have gone back and forth at will."

"Weren't you afraid that Frau Helriegel would post a guard?" I was running out of questions. The answer to this one was obvious.

"Do you think she wanted the cops to know about her vault?" he said. Picking up another key, he looked at it, turning it over. He smiled and pocketed this one. "Okay, ladies, this is it," he announced, coming around the desk to block any escape route we might be contemplating. "I'm going to solve all your problems. Sit in the chairs at the desk." He gestured with the gun.

"Are you going to shoot us? Just like that?" I gasped.

"Yeah, I'm in a hurry. So, sit down," he ordered callously.

I couldn't move. I stared at him, as he pulled out his handy ever-present role of duct tape. The duct tape had somehow become a label for Mark and his crew. It's amazing how some part of my brain finds humor in these situations. I guess it's the mind's escape key.

"Look, Mark. We won't say anything. You were never here, Okay?" Francesca said in a pleading voice.

His eyes flashed at her as if to say, "Fat chance." Holding the gun on us, he made Francesca tape my mouth. Then I had to do hers.

"Stand up, bitches," he snarled, making me tape Francesca's hands behind her back. When I finished, he pushed her onto the floor and then taped my hands. I thought about my cellphone in the pocket of my coat. Not the slimmest chance of using that phone either I realized, feeling panic rise.

Our chance to beg for mercy was also gone. I couldn't even warn him about Frank Caputo who was supposed to be on his way.

"Okay, head for the kitchen in the back, and no funny stuff." He yanked Francesca off the floor with one hand, poking me in the back with the gun.

Once in the kitchen Mark shoved us each into a chair on opposite sides of the room. He pulled out some rope from a broom closet and tied us to the chairs, using those special knots that only tighten with resistance.

He leered at us, "Too bad I'm in such a hurry. I would have liked to have had a little fun with you two before I offed you. I get off on fear."

My stomach lurched. He disgusted me, and more than that, I couldn't believe we would be lucky enough to escape a second time. I looked at Francesca. Her dark eyes seemed to send a laser message of hatred and revulsion. When she turned to look at me, the laser beam faded to tears. I could read the silent message, "I'm sorry!"

Mark walked out of the room. *Was that it,* I thought. *He's just going to leave us like this? He's not going to shoot us?* I could hear him in the other rooms, the click of his heels going from room to room. *What is he doing?*

When he entered the conservatory I could hear him rattling the glass doors. He returned to the kitchen, announcing, "All locked up and safe!" He flashed that familiar evil grin that twisted his face into a menacing mask.

He busied himself rummaging through the kitchen drawers, two sets of panic-stricken eyes following his every move. He found some emergency candles and went into the small dinette adjoining the kitchen. He lit them, let the wax drip onto some paper plates from the counter and affixed the candles to the plates. There were six candles in all. Was Mark into satanic rituals? Confusion was becoming a constant companion.

He came back into the kitchen and turned on all the gas jets at the range and the oven, leaving its door ajar. He blew out the flames, letting the gas escape freely.

"Bye, bye, ladies." He hurried out the back door locking it behind him.

For a stunned few seconds, Francesca and I just stared at each other.

Oh, God, think! I can't die like this. My brain demanded action. I looked at Francesca through my tears and saw that she was rocking her chair towards me. I began to do the same. We inched closer to each other as the gas began to fill the room.

I tried to remember if natural gas was heavier or lighter than air. If we fell over would we be safer? If the gas blew up and we survived the impact, would we miss being burned to death or would the explosion use up all the oxygen?

Francesca was gesturing with her head. I got it. We needed to be back to back to try to untie each other's hands. We got into position, and tried to reach each other from behind. My arms are so much longer than Francesca's that I could reach her fingers. I gripped the tape and slipped. I tried again, and slipped. I felt Francesca's nails dig into my exposed palm. She fumbles for the end of the tape.

The gas smell was getting worse. Then I remembered that natural gas is lighter than air. It floats. My chemistry teacher used to fill soap bubbles from the gas jets in the lab, and as they floated up, ignite them. They didn't explode, just burned really hot.

Francesca was making progress. I could hear the rasp of tape being pulled off, but my hands were not free. I tugged. I was able to wiggle my wrists enough to grab onto Francesca's tape again and pull. More ripping. Francesca got one hand free. She pulled at my tape. We worked together instinctively knowing when to be still so the other could work the tape, and when to struggle against the tape. It is amazing what a little adrenalin can do.

With hands free, we needed to work on the ropes, but as I pulled, the knots tightened. My eyes were tearing badly now and so were Francesca's. She was very red in the face, trying to cough through the tape. Maybe if we fell over on the chairs they would break and we could wriggle out of the ropes.

Francesca's head fell against her chest which was heaving visibly. I moaned through the tape to get her attention. She shook her head signaling resignation.

Panic welled up from my gut. I watched the six wavering flames in the next room. The gas continued to hiss its noxious fumes. I was feeling nauseous from the gas. As I tried desperately to come up with another plan, the candles in the next room blurred. In one last effort I lurched in my chair and crashed into Francesca's. We both went crashing to the floor, breaking the chairs, as I had hoped. Francesca was not moving. My hearing kept fading in and out like bad radio reception.

No cellphone! No Aunt J! No Frank Caputo! Just the awful gas and those six candles. I tried to move my legs. Was

I dreaming? No, I wiggled free of the chair. I tried struggling to my feet. No luck. Think! What to do first. The candles! No candles, no flame, no explosion.

I couldn't stand, but I could drag myself to the dinette. I couldn't reach high enough to blow out the candles. Again, the only thing I could do was to topple the table. It was one of those foldable ones, and a flimsy one at that. I lurched my body into the table legs. It teetered. One more violent lurch, and the table toppled.

Three candles died. One had gone out on its own. There were still two pools of burning wax. Lurch, lurch, lurch! I fell on the puddles, rolling as best I could to keep my clothes from catching fire. I was so dizzy. No explosion now, just asphyxiation from the gas.

Francesca! Was she dead? The lights went out and it became silent. But then they went on again. *I'm losing consciousness!* Panic was my only real feeling now. The lights went out again, but did I hear another sound? Like wind chimes. Tinkle, tinkle. Did they have wind chimes in heaven? The panic receded as I drifted again.

A loud splintering shattered the silence. Glass shattering! Where? Did the gas explode anyway? I felt strong hands drag me. Oh no, Mark is back. He is going to "have some fun" with me. I felt the tape being ripped from my mouth and strong arms lifted me. I didn't care anymore. Cold air washed over me. I gulped it in, the air more important than my fear of Mark.

"Francesca?" I rasped.

"We've got her," said a stranger's voice. My head started to clear, but I was so nauseous. My leg was killing me. *What had just happened?*

I woke up in another E.R. *This is getting old*, I thought as Aunt J's head emerged from the murk of my vision.

"You really need to convince this Frank Caputo to get the lead out, J." I smiled at the grim teary face of Aunt J, hoping she would get my joke.

She grabbed my hand, squeezing tight and turning her head to get control. "I nearly lost you, little Annie. I can never let that happen." My aunt's big heart had taken over her big self-control. I loved her for that. I squeezed back.

"I love you, Auntie. I guess we just must continue to save each other." She put her head next to mine on the bed and we cried together. I was safe at last.

"Francesca?" I looked at her fearing the worst.

"Falling over to the floor in the chair saved her life. Natural gas rises and the good air at floor level revived her enough to hang on until the marines arrived. You both will be here overnight."

"Mark DiCristiani?" Another question.

"We're working on it. Get some rest. There's a police officer outside your room and Francesca's too. I will pick you up in the morning, if they let me. I've got to get back to the investigation."

"Get him, J. He's not finished doing bad things. I'll tell you about his threats later." She left and I tried to get the images of the last twelve hours out of my head.

Chapter 17
THE SATURDAY ART CLASS

AUNT J, TRUE TO HER word, picked us up at the hospital the next morning.

"Did you find Mark DiCristiani?" Francesca asked nervously. She was truly the worse for wear, both eyes blackened from her fall in the chair and pale from the near asphyxiation. Both our lips were torn from the tape, and I had a bad bruise on my leg from my fall with the chair.

"We're working on it," Aunt J replied tersely. She related to us the state of the search for Mark. They were able to get the key number from a list that Francesca had found and filed a few days ago. Thanks to her meticulous filing system, the detectives were able to check out the list and locate the possibilities for safe deposit keys and the banks where they could be found. The banks were being watched, the bank managers alerted and aware of the dangerous nature of anyone trying to access certain safe deposit boxes. So far, Mark DiCristiani seemed to have gone underground.

Francesca was very quiet, looking small in the corner of the back seat. "He's tried twice to kill us. They say third time's a charm," she said morosely.

I couldn't blame her for feeling that way. I was scared too, but I had faith in Aunt J and the rest of the N.Y.P.D.

"Francesca, we will not leave you or Annie without protection until he's caught. I realize now just how cunning he is, and how motivated by hate." Aunt J set her jaw firmly. I knew that look, and I couldn't help but feel safer.

Francesca stirred, seeming to respond to Aunt J's latest attempt to put her mind at rest.

"Paolo invited us for dinner last night, just before Mark showed up. Max and Frieda prepared a pot roast and a little celebration," I said.

"I know. I had your phone tapped," she replied. "Some of my surveillance worked." Aunt J continued, "I called Max and Frieda to see if they would give us a rain check for tonight, and the answer was an enthusiastic yes."

I was glad we were going to have a pot roast dinner with a group of people. I needed something normal. I was beginning to feel like I'd spent the last few days on a movie set. Home-cooked reality was what we all needed.

We arrived at the brownstone. Max and Frieda met us at the door. "You look awful," they gasped.

"Good evening Frauline Tillery," they added, nodding to Aunt J, their manners always correct. "The Frau and young Paolo are vaiting for you inside. Ve vere so vorried."

We followed them into the kitchen where Paolo and his grandmother were snacking on hors d'oeuvres.

"Before I got the call from Miss Tillery, I was about to call out the national guard," Paolo said, taking a closer look at us. "I see he didn't go without a fight." he frowned at Francesca's black eyes.

"Why did he take the chance of coming back?" asked Frau Helriegel.

"He returned to get a key. Unfortunately, he found the girls as well."

"Please fill us in on the details," said Paolo trying to get his crutches under him to take a closer look at us.

"Frau Helriegel and Paolo, you know what happened at the gallery. The Fire Department filled you in. You are beginning to know the firemen so well that you might have to invite them for Thanksgiving dinner." We laughed at Aunt J's joke, and she related the current state of affairs regarding Mark and the safe deposit box.

"How did you get hurt Francesca?" Paolo asked gently.

"The usual," she replied. "I think Mark wants me to like him. Every time I see him, he tries to make an impression on me. He's just a little rough around the edges." She smiled at her own humor.

Aunt J elaborated more seriously, "He was going to complete the job he started on the bridge. He almost succeeded."

The reality of another narrow escape caused my heart to do flip flops.

Paolo signaled to Max. "Can you get my doctor's bag from my room, please? I'd like to see to Francesca's head wound."

The budding doctor gave Francesca a quick exam, satisfying himself that she would survive. Every eye in the room was on Francesca and me. I could read the emotions in their faces, concern, fear, admiration.

"You two sure can keep your heads in a dangerous situation. You went a long way toward saving your own lives," Aunt J stated. Francesca blushed. I thanked my guardian angel for remembering all that good stuff she and my father had taught me since I was a very small kid.

We sat at the large kitchen table and devoured the lovely pot roast dinner, hungry as bears after our ordeal. The meal helped us relax, the homey atmosphere and good food making us feel safe and normal.

As we dug into dessert, the door bell rang. It was Lt. Red. After a round of hugging, kisses, and handshaking, he told us the rest of the story.

"I thought you girls would like to know, we have Mark in custody and the other man from the bridge as well. You know, the one who got away? The judge won't hear a plea for bail until tomorrow morning for either of them."

"He'll get out on bail?" Paolo was incredulous.

"He'll try," Lt. Red laughed. "Having attempted murder twice, he won't be granted bail."

"How did you get him?" Francesca asked.

It was the safe deposit key," Red explained. "Just as we hoped, he showed up at one of the banks we were watching. We'll find out what's in it tomorrow. We expect its money he would have used for a getaway."

"Wouldn't he have been stopped at the bank?" I asked.

"Maybe, but his being wanted by the police hasn't been widely advertised. And, if the box is under another name, with a slightly altered appearance, it would be easy for him to slip in, pick up his money, and slip out again. We needed to put specific boxes under surveillance." Aunt J explained.

Lt. Red beamed at us, continuing his commentary. "We had another break in the arson case. That matchbook you picked up in the basement is going to be a key piece of evidence."

"How so?" I asked, trying to keep pride from my voice.

"The arson investigators found some half-burned matches near the fuse device used to set the fire. Upon microscopic examination, the torn ends exactly fit the spaces for the missing matches in the matchbook that you found, Annie. There was a partial thumb print on the book as well. Our latent's expert is working on a match with one of our suspects."

"What about the phone number on the matchbook?" I asked.

"It was traced to a beeper. It belonged to your bridge buddy, the one with the broken back," Red replied.

"It sounds like our three kidnappers will be sent away for a good long time," Aunt J said, sounding pleased.

"Any news of my Uncle Horst?" Paolo asked, keeping his voice level.

"None. We did find a small black book in the office at the gallery."

"I must have dropped it when I got knocked out," Francesca offered.

"We've been meaning to look through it as well." Red smiled. "We're checking out the names and phone numbers.

I have a feeling it'll be a very enlightening glimpse into the underworld."

"Well, I have had some very good news. At least, for me and for others, I hope," Frau Helriegel offered tentatively, speaking for the first time since Lt. Red had arrived. All eyes turned her way.

"I spoke to my lawyers today. I would like to clear my conscience. I am an old woman. I have made an offer to the prosecutor. I have established a scholarship fund from the money I made from the sale of some of the original paintings that were my lover's gift from so long ago. With that fortune, I have created a fund for young artists who have shown talent. They are to receive lessons, and my gallery will be used to showcase their paintings."

"This foundation will also pay the salary of a qualified person to oversee the operation. Paolo's mother will be in charge of the entire operation. I would like my first recipient to be Miss Francesca Gabrielli." Frau Helriegel smiled at the end of her disclosure, seeming very satisfied with her proposal.

Francesca gasped. Her benefactor continued, "This will give you fewer responsibilities at the gallery, and more time to study. I hope you will use it wisely."

Francesca got up and hugged Frau Helriegel, tears welling in her eyes. A round of congratulations and approving comments buzzed around the room for the next few minutes.

"Will Francesca still run the art classes," I asked. "She is my favorite teacher," I added, hoping I would not lose her entirely to her own studies.

"I was looking forward to my Saturday art class," Francesca offered looking speculatively at Frau Helriegel.

"I think that is your decision, Francesca," Frau Helriegel replied.

"Oh, I definitely want to continue giving lessons. Look at the fun I've had as a result of them," she quipped, making a face and rubbing her head.

"Good!" I chimed in. "You do have a knack for adding a certain element of excitement to your teaching, Miss Gabrielli. I can't wait to see what tomorrow's lesson might bring!" I winked at Aunt J, who shot back, "Just keep that special cell phone handy, and remember where old number 7 is!"

"What happened to that special cellphone, Miss Tillery?" Francesca asked.

"I've made duplicates. Both of you will have one, and call me Aunt J, please."

We said our goodbyes. Aunt J put her arm around my shoulders as and we left Francesca with the Helriegels, and headed for home.

"Annie, there was a phone message from Ty on the answering machine. I forgot to tell you."

"That's odd. Why didn't he just leave a message on my cell?"

"I don't know, but I think it might be something he wants both of us to talk to him about," Aunt J offered.

"Hmmm. Another mystery for us to solve?"

Aunt J smiled and winked at me, tightening her grip.